I was just about to turn back when I saw two horses and a wagon coming my way.

I pulled my suitcases to the side of the road and grabbed my hat before another gust of wind blew it away. It whipped at my long skirt beneath my coat and I wished that I had worn something warmer.

I watched the horse and wagon slowly approach. Someone was terribly confused about what a carriage was. This was a wagon. The kind people used in the western movies.

The driver, wearing a heavy coat and hat, stopped just after the two horses passed me.

"Hello," he said, tipping his hat at me.

"Hi," I said, holding my own hat to keep it from flying off, and looking up at the ruggedly handsome man with gritty stubble. If he was going for the dangerous western gunslinger look, he had it pegged.

He was grinning at me and for some reason, that irritated me.

MOUNTBATTEN PINK

ALSO BY KATHRYN KALEIGH

THE BECQUERELS
Time Travel Romance

Dragon's Blood

Lavender Blue

Champagne Silver

Twilight Frost

Mountbatten Pink

Written in the Wind

Scripted in the Stars

Destined in the Twilight

Promised in the Mist

Trapped in the Melody

Twist of Fate

When the Stars Align

Once in a Blue Moon

Once Upon a Christmas

A Wish Upon a Star

When Lightning Strikes

Storm of Time

Midnight Storm

When the Moon Falls

Stormborn Angel

Time Tempest

The Heart Remembers

A Moment in Time

Moonlight Shadows

Rescued in Time

Falling Through to Forever

MOUNTBATTEN PINK

THE BECQUERELS

KATHRYN KALEIGH

MOUNTBATTEN PINK

PREVIEW: THE HEART OF CHRISTMAS

To learn more about Kathryn Kaleigh, visit

www.kathrynkaleigh.com

Kathryn Kaleigh

1

———

ISABELLA BECQUEREL

Today

$\mathcal{M}$E: *I'm here.*

After texting Thomas, I tucked my phone into the pocket of my long light brown wool coat.

"This is it," the cab driver said with a thick accent.

"This is what?" I asked, looking out the windows for any sign of the Daniels House hotel.

"You wait here for carriage," he said in what he obviously thought was for clarification.

I shook my head and made no move to open the door.

The cab driver watched me in the rearview mirror for about five seconds, then got out and opened my door.

"There's nothing here," I insisted, not budging.

"Carriage Stop," he said, leaving the door open and going around to open the trunk. He pulled out my two big suitcases and set them on the ground.

"No… Ugh." Bringing my leather laptop messenger bag and my LV handbag with me, I slid out of the cab.

The driver rolled my luggage over to what he called the Carriage Stop, then circled back to close my door.

"Have good trip," he said, getting into the driver's seat and driving off. I watched the cab's brake lights as he followed the sharp downhill curve and disappeared the way we had just come.

A burst of cold wind, coming off rugged Rocky Mountain peaks towering in every direction swept through the valley.

My messenger bag over one shoulder, my handbag over the other, I held onto my burgundy cloche hat and turned my back to the wind.

The cab driver had left me here in the middle of nowhere. I had booked him to take me to the Daniels House hotel. Not to leave me—and my two bags of luggage—on the side of the road.

I'll take care of this. I'll just report him. I took my phone out of my pocket and unlocked it.

No service.

Seriously? I had just texted Thomas. I pulled up his message. *Message not delivered.*

I was literally out here alone with no cell phone service.

Turning, I glared at the wooden bench serving as what looked more like a resting stop in a park than a bus stop.

I sat on the cold bench and crossed my arms, choosing mad over scared.

June in the mountains of Colorado was a lot colder than I expected. It had been sweltering hot for months already in Houston. And to think I had only brought my coat because Thomas told me about a hundred times that I would need it.

He was right about that. But I was not convinced that he was right that this trip was a good idea.

Ten months of face-time calls, texts, and emails after three years of dating.

He'd followed a new job from Houston to San Francisco and I had stayed in Houston where I had a perfectly good office and a long waiting list of clients.

I'd asked Thomas to come visit me in Houston. Offered to visit him in San Francisco.

But… no. I liked to consider myself flexible, so I'd gone along with this trip to Colorado.

It'll be fun.

You'll love it.

It's beautiful.

I had translated that into romantic. Figured we would decide what we were going to do about our relationship. We couldn't keep going like this. Not seeing each other for ten months.

Our holiday trip had fallen through. Something to do with his sister.

It wasn't a huge deal. The holidays had been a busy time of year for me, too, so I had let it slide.

Thomas and I had been together for three years, starting in college. We had a history together. That was supposed to mean something.

I looked off to my left. The Daniels House was supposed to be right up the road, tucked at the top of the mountains in a nest of fir and spruce trees. They touted unparalleled views. Exquisite cuisine. Personalized service.

Maybe I would just walk the rest of the way. I did not need a carriage to take me to the hotel. I adjusted my bags, grabbed a suitcase with each hand and took five steps.

They could have sprung a bit to make themselves a decent road. The road was nothing more than a wide walking path. No wonder they didn't allow cars up here. They didn't want the liability.

I was wearing boots, but city hiking boots, not country hiking boots.

This was not going to work.

I looked over my shoulder. There were snow clouds coming in.

The only reason I knew this was because I had visited my brother in Salt Lake City for Christmas two years ago. Instead of a mild Texas holiday, I had experienced a winter storm that had delayed my flight home for three days.

I was just about to turn back when I saw two horses and a wagon coming my way.

I pulled my suitcases to the side of the road and grabbed my hat before another gust of wind blew it away. It whipped at my long skirt beneath my coat and I wished that I had worn something warmer.

I watched the horse and wagon slowly approach. Someone was terribly confused about what a carriage was. This was a wagon. The kind people used in the western movies.

The driver, wearing a heavy coat and hat, stopped just after the two horses passed me.

"Hello," he said, tipping his hat at me.

"Hi," I said, holding my own hat to keep it from flying off, and looking up at the ruggedly handsome man with gritty stubble. If he was going for the dangerous western gunslinger look, he had it pegged.

He was grinning at me and for some reason, that irritated me.

2

COLTON AUCLAIR

1870

There was a storm coming and being the only single man on what we'd started calling the hill, I was elected by default to go into Whiskey Springs for supplies.

One of my sisters had an infant and the other one had one on the way, so it was understandable that their husbands didn't want to leave them. Not one of them had a problem sending their brother into town.

Not that I minded getting out in the fresh air.

I whistled to myself as I made my way along the road leading to town. It was downhill all the way and uphill all the way back. I wasn't sure which was worse and I was pretty sure the horses didn't care for either.

But they were two good horses and didn't complain. One of them, in fact, was a war horse I'd bought off a fellow who'd fought in the war.

If the war had gone on for just one more year, I would have

been in there. Like every other southern man worth his salt, fighting my way through a lost cause.

But fortunately or unfortunately, depending on which way the wind blew, the war had ended and I had come to Whiskey Springs with my four sisters.

Not only was I the middle child, I was the only boy out of five siblings. It was easy enough for a sane man to understand why I had been itching to join the army. I had still not ruled out joining the United States Cavalry.

I saw the girl standing there as I made my way around one of the switchbacks that made the trip downhill about a hundred percent safer, but I figured it was just a trick of the light.

The road between my sisters' houses and Whiskey Springs was deserted to say the least.

My brother-in-law, Graham, owned the whole mountain, so unless he had sold land to someone, this was all private property. I had it on good authority that that wasn't going to be happening anytime soon. Graham had every intention of passing along an unparalleled huge estate to his heirs.

Since his wife was already expecting her second child, he was obviously quite serious about that. He claimed that this land would increase exponentially in value over the next few hundred years.

Personally, I was more of a here and now kind of person. Since I had no heirs and no signs of any in my future, I didn't have to worry anyone other than myself.

About ninety percent of the time I was more than okay with that.

As I came around the curve, fully expecting the image of the young lady to have vanished, I saw her standing there looking quite vexed.

There were so many things wrong with this picture. First, she wasn't dressed properly for this kind of weather.

Second, she should not be out here alone. This country was still wild and there were men who would want to do her harm. My youngest sister, Elise, had gone through an encounter with such a man just last December, so I was more than aware of such things.

And third, she just looked so completely out of place. A woman standing on the edge of a mountain cliff with a stack of luggage looking completely lost.

I had four sisters. I knew when a girl was putting on a brave face.

I stopped the horses just as I reached her.

"Mind if I ask what you're doing out here?" I asked.

"Waiting for the..." She waved a hand in frustration. "Carriage to take me up to the house."

"The carriage—" Someone had sorely misled this girl. "Are you alone?"

She rolled her eyes at me. She was from the city, I decided. She had that sophisticated look about her. My sister, Bailey was going to love this lady's clothes. Bailey liked to keep up with the latest fashion.

"I'm Colton," I said. "I can take you up to the house."

"No," she said. "I'll just wait for the carriage."

Locking the wagon wheels, I climbed down and stood in front of her.

She had the most beautiful green eyes I had ever seen. With the late evening sunlight reflecting in her eyes, I saw little shards of dark green, light green, and the tiniest little gold sparkle.

Her heart-shaped face was classically perfect. And her bow-shaped lips begged to be kissed, even as she scowled at me.

"There is no carriage," I said.

"I was assured—"

I picked up one of her trunks and tossed it into the back of the wagon.

"Wait."

I picked up the other one and tossed it in back, too.

"What?" I asked. "You want to just stand out here for some mythical carriage? Sorry. I can't let you do it. You'll freeze to death. And there are wild animals."

She rubbed her arms and glanced around, her eyes wide now.

"I can walk," she said, but there was no conviction in her voice.

I took her big leather bag, put I over my own shoulder, then held out a hand to help her onto the wagon.

She just looked blankly at me.

This girl had no idea how to climb onto a wagon.

She screeched when I picked her up and set her unceremoniously on the wagon seat. She didn't weigh more than a sack of potatoes, but she smelled a whole lot better. Like a meadow of spring flowers.

"My hat," she said.

I looked down at her burgundy hat. Picked it up, dusted it off, and handed it to her.

I noticed, as I went around to get on the wagon, that she did not put it back on her head. She just held it in her lap.

"Where are we going?" she asked as we started moving forward.

"I have to turn this Titanic around," I said.

"Fine," she said, crossing her arms and staring straight ahead.

I grinned as I used a wide place in the trail to turn the horses and wagon around.

This woman had passion and grit. Something I'd had a hard time finding in any girl outside of family. She also had a hint of that southern accent that reminded me of home.

I was intrigued.

When I had us pointed in the right direction to go home, I took off my gloves and handed them her.

"Put these on," I said.

My sisters would have to do without their provisions for another day.

3

———

ISABELLA

We rode in the wagon for twenty minutes. Maybe thirty. Twenty minutes of bumpy, cold travel.

It only took one good bump of gripping the wooden seat with my bare hands for me to, however reluctantly, put Colton's gloves on.

I shoved the hat on my head and gripped the wooden seat to keep myself from being tossed off.

I could already see that I was going to have to give the Daniels House credit for the views they claimed to have.

But the impeccable service? Not so much.

I was already writing the review in my head.

The cab driver dumped me out on the side of the road and told me to wait for a carriage. The so-called carriage was a man driving a wooden wagon.

I looked over at the man who introduced himself as Colton.

A smart person would not have gotten in the wagon with him. But I had been caught between a rock and a hard place.

He had been right about my choices. Either go with him or stand out here and freeze. Or maybe worse…be eaten by wild animals. I'd seen the movies with the bears and the wolves. The wild animals do not play. That was the lesson I had taken from what Thomas had called entertaining movies. Personally, I preferred a good drama. Romances were okay, too.

"How long were you out there?" he asked. "Waiting?"

"I don't know," I said. "A few minutes."

"Did you walk from town… or…?" he looked at me curiously.

I guess he was just trying to make conversation. And he was trying to be kind, so I tried not to be prickly. It wasn't his fault this was happening.

"I caught a ride," I said. "I didn't know he was going to dump me off in the middle of nowhere."

"You have to be careful," he said. "I'd advise you not to go off with strangers."

I gave him a look that made him laugh.

"What?" he asked, not bothering to try to keep a straight face.

"You're a stranger."

He shrugged and adjusted the reins he held lightly in his hands.

I would have felt a bit safer if he had held those reins a little bit more tightly.

Following along the gently rising switchbacks, we circled around, going up and up in elevation.

I adjusted his gloves that were almost falling off my hands.

It was quite intimate wearing his gloves and I would have given that more thought except that right about then the Daniels House came into view.

Pictures did not do it justice. The house was four stories tall with tons of big windows to let in light from any direction. The top floor was probably two-thirds all windows. Lots of chimneys.

In fact, the number of chimneys, all billowing smoke, seemed to be one of its defining features. That and its windows. It was an interesting combination.

To say that it was impressive was an understatement.

The house looked surprisingly well-kept. New even. If I hadn't known the house had been built in the 1860s, I would have thought it was no more than a couple of years old.

It was amazing what a fresh coat of paint could do.

I remembered reading that no cars were allowed at the house. I remembered it because it reminded me of one of my favorite places, Mackinac Island. No cars there either.

In fact, I now remembered Thomas calling this the Mackinac of the west. I hadn't paid much attention to him. I had been secretly hoping I could change his mind and get him to meet in Denver instead.

But now that I was here, I had to admit that I was impressed.

It was even more breathtaking because now that we were on top of the mountain, there were clouds below us.

That was something I had never seen, except of course, other than from an airplane.

But being here, in this high elevation, with the clouds below us, I felt a little breathless. Maybe it was the stress. Maybe it was the elevation. Or a little bit of both.

Colton must have noticed.

After securing the brake on the wagon, he looked over at me.

"Take slow, deep breaths," he said.

I nodded. And attempted to do just that.

But the way he was looking at me was not helping.

My breath actually started to come in shorter and more shallow.

He put a hand on my chest, just below my neck.

"Breath with me," he said, his eyes locking onto mine.

I did. I breathed with him. Slow and deep.

But my heart was beating too fast. It wasn't the elevation now. It was Colton and his hand on my chest. It was his sapphire-blue eyes locked onto mine.

Finally, I began to settle.

"We're here," he said.

I nodded. "Okay."

"Let's get you inside to a warm fire."

"Yes," I said. "Let's." That was about all the brain power I had at this point.

With a smile, he jumped down from the wagon and walked around to my side.

He did not even hesitate this time. He just picked me up and hauled me off the wagon. He set my feet on the ground, but didn't let go of my arms.

I gasped, but did not screech this time.

"Get your footing," he said.

"I'm fine," I said.

He removed his hand and I swayed. Just a little, but his hand was immediately back on my arms.

He tucked my left hand into the crook of his elbow and escorted me up the stairs, across the veranda lined with over half a dozen white rocking chairs and in through the magnificent front door.

The house was impressive.

Two-story high ceilings in the foyer. Two staircases that intersected at the top with a wide balcony.

A tall grandfather clock stood right in the center of the foyer, between the two stairways, cheerfully ticking away the minutes.

An oversized fireplace was the centerpiece of the wall to the left. A comfortable sofa and two chairs in front of it.

"You can sit over here," Colton said, leading me toward that sitting area. "I'll bring your trunks."

He didn't leave me until I was seated. *My trunks.*

This Colton fellow was disarming.

I had to admit I found him rather likeable.

4

COLTON

Taking the steps two at the time, I jogged up to my sister's studio on the fourth floor of the house.

Bailey, wearing an apron splattered with a hundred different colors over her long, belled-out dress, wielded a paint brush. Dakota, big as a house, awaiting the impending birth of her first child, sat in front of the fireplace, her fingers moving with knitting needles.

They both looked up when I stepped into the room.

"What are you doing back?" Bailey asked.

"I didn't go," I said, going to stand in front of the fire next to Dakota.

"Why not?" Dakota asked, looking toward the windows to see if the storm had come in sooner than expected.

"We have a guest," I said.

"Who is it?" Dakota asked, her brow creasing.

"Who?" Bailey asked, setting her brush down and coming toward us.

It was odd. Dakota's response was suspicious while Bailey's was interested. But that was typical of my sisters. Bailey would be happy with a house full of people at any given time whereas

Dakota would be content to live with only her husband. Family was okay, but anyone else she could do without.

"A young lady," I said.

Dakota went back to her knitting, resigning herself to having someone else around.

"What's her name?" Bailey asked.

I looked at Bailey sideways. "I don't know."

Bailey laughed. "You brought home a stranger."

"She was standing at the overlook with her trunks," I said. "I couldn't leave her there."

"That's odd," Bailey said.

"Could have asked for her name," Dakota said, mostly to herself.

"It didn't matter who she is," I insisted. "I still couldn't leave her there."

"You did the right thing," Bailey decided. "I'll go down and welcome her."

"No need for all that," I said. "Don't stop painting. I've got this."

"You sure?" Bailey asked.

"I'm positive."

"Okay," Bailey, obviously disappointed, went back to her painting. "Put her on the third floor."

"Got it," I said. "Just wanted to let you know that you'll have to wait until the storm passes to get the supplies."

As I headed out, my thoughts racing with what all I needed to do, I heard my sisters talking.

"We really needed the supplies," Dakota said.

"We'll get them later," Bailey said. "The storm is coming in hard."

I stopped by the third floor and slid the girl's trunks from the hallway into the room next to mine.

Then I closed the door to what was currently my bedroom, and headed back down to the first floor.

The girl... I couldn't believe I hadn't even asked for her name... sat in front of the fireplace where I had left her.

I was struck again by how beautiful she was. Elegant.

She sat straight on the edge of the chair, staring into the flames.

I found myself wondering what she was thinking about.

She had removed her hat and her dark hair framed her face in loose waves.

She looked up when she saw me and waited until I sat on the sofa across from her.

"I'm supposed to meet someone," she said.

"Who?" I was thinking perhaps she was talking about one of my sisters, probably Bailey. Bailey had talked about taking on a couple of young artists as students. Not for the money, just for the challenge.

"Thomas Richards," she said, looking up at me expectantly. "Has he made it yet?"

I slowly shook my head. "I don't think so."

"Could you check?" she asked. "I was actually running late, so he should be here."

"There's no one here by that name," I said.

"Oh." She lowered her gaze, her brow furrowed.

"My apologies," he said. "But I didn't ask your name."

"Isabella," she said. "Isabella Becquerel."

5

ISABELLA

"Becquerel?" Colton asked, like he didn't believe me.

"Yes," I said. "Do you think I could go ahead and go to my room?"

I was somewhat reluctant to leave the warm fire with the crackling logs—real logs. Not gas logs. There was a stack of firewood a few paces away from the fireplace.

The house was quiet. Other than the cozy sounds of the fireplace and the steady ticking of the grandfather clock, it was perfectly quiet. No background music. No people talking.

Was this an off season?

If so, that would explain a whole lot of things.

But I was pretty sure that summer was a prime time for tourists.

"Of course," Colton said, still looking warily at me as he stood up. "I'll show you upstairs to your room."

I followed him across the open foyer to the staircase on the left.

Then he gestured for me to go up the stairs ahead of him.

After taking a couple of steps up, I had to stop and catch my breath.

"It's the elevation," he said. "You really should get some rest."

"I will," I promised. I took two more steps and stopped again. The weakness was almost overwhelming and the nausea didn't help. "How much further?"

"Your room is on the third floor."

"Oh," I said. "There's no elevator?"

"Elevator? Hardly."

"It's okay," I said. "I can make it."

"Seriously," he said. "You should rest downstairs."

I waved him off. "I need to be alone. To make some calls." Maybe take a nap.

But my heart was beating too fast and I was short of breath.

"You're from the south," he said.

I nodded. I ran five miles a day. I was in good shape.

"This happened to my younger sister," he said.

"How long does it last?" I asked.

"You'll feel better by tomorrow," he said.

"I hope so."

"If not," he said. "You may have to go back down to Whiskey Springs."

That wasn't such a bad idea, but now that I was here, I sort of liked it and wanted to enjoy it. With or without Thomas.

I took my time walking up the stairs and Colton didn't rush me.

I'd read that the Daniels House was a family-owned business. Owned and run by family.

"Are you one of the owners?" I asked as we reached the first landing. Halfway to the second floor.

"My sister and her husband own the house," he said. "I'm just visiting."

I nodded. Wondered vaguely if this was a panic attack. I'd never had one, but my symptoms fit all the criteria.

By the time we got to the second floor, I didn't think I could go on.

"I think I'll just rest here," I said. I must have swayed a bit.

Without a word, Colton picked me up, one arm under my legs and the other supporting my back. I wrapped my arms around his neck and held on as he carried me up the next set of stairs to the third floor.

After I decided he wasn't going to drop me, I closed my eyes and rested my cheek on his shoulder. He smelled good. Like outdoors after a rain storm.

I opened my eyes as he carried me right into a room and deposited me on a four-poster bed. My suitcases, or trunks as he called them, sat neatly next to the bed.

"I'll be right back," he said.

Curious about what he was doing next, I sat on the edge of the bed and looked around the room as I waited. The large bed had green velvet curtains tied at each of the four bedposts. The curtains matched the ones at the windows that were pulled back to give a splendid view of the mountain peaks in the distance.

There was a fireplace between the two windows—corresponding with one of the many chimneys I had seen from outside.

There was a wardrobe and a lady's vanity with a mirror and stool.

Otherwise, there was an interesting en suite bathroom. The old-fashioned clawfoot tub sat out in the middle of the floor.

Colton came back with a pitcher of water and a glass. He filled the glass with water and handed it to me.

Maybe the service wasn't so bad here, after all, at the Daniels House hotel.

6

COLTON

I found Graham sitting in his study reading a newspaper, his feet propped on his desk.

Graham had this study and he had one on the fourth floor where he could be near his wife. But lately, he'd been giving the two sisters some time by themselves.

This study had nothing in it other than a desk, his chair, and a bookcase full of books. The walls, of course, were covered in Bailey Auclair's paintings.

When he had built the house shortly after their wedding, he had challenged her to paper the walls with her paintings. She was making progress in that direction.

And she was good. I had to admit it, even if she was my sister. She mostly did landscapes and wildlife. There were certainly enough breathtaking views from here to keep her busy. Every season. Every day. Sometimes even different times of day looked different.

Lowering the newspaper, he looked up. "Did you know they finished the transcontinental railroad?" he asked. "Drove what they called a gold spike in the ground in Utah."

"You don't say," I said, sliding into a chair on the other side of his desk.

"You said it would happen," I said.

"True." Graham was fascinated by history. He claimed to enjoy *seeing it unfold in front of his eyes.*

Of course, the thing that was hard to forget was that Graham already knew what the next century held.

Our immediate family members were the only ones who knew that Graham was from the twenty-first century.

After accidentally finding a portal into the past, he had chosen to stay here in the past to live his life with my sister Bailey.

Graham was an anomaly. After losing his entire family in an airplane crash, he had turned his insurance money into little gold bars which he had brought with him to the past.

That made him one of the richest men in the country. He bought himself a mountain, built himself a castle, and lived quietly with his family.

He was not only the richest man I had ever met, he was hands down the happiest.

His cheerfulness had a tendency to be contagious.

Graham set the paper aside. "I heard we have an unexpected guest."

"We do. A young lady."

An unexpected guest was rare. Graham and Bailey sometimes held parties here at their home, but as far as I knew, no one ever came up here without an invitation.

Until now.

"Where is she?"

"Resting. Elevation sickness."

"That's unfortunate. Tell me about her."

"She was standing at the overlook. Said someone just dropped her off there and she was waiting for a carriage."

"Seems strange."

"She wasn't dressed right," I said. "Just a long coat and… her skirt was short. A riding habit, maybe?"

Graham dropped his feet onto the floor and leaned forward. "How short?"

"A few inches above her ankles. She was wearing boots, so it wasn't really noticeable."

"What else?"

"Said she was supposed to be meeting someone else here. And." I replayed my conversation with her. "Said she had to make some calls."

"I need to see her," Graham said.

"She was really disoriented, Graham," I said. "Bad elevation sickness. She should be better tomorrow, right?"

"May have to take her back down to Whiskey Springs," he said, but he wasn't really looking for an answer.

Graham opened a sketch pad to a blank sheet of paper and, using a pencil, quickly sketched out two figures. He admittedly wasn't much of an artist.

He pointed to the first figure. "This is how our girls look, right?"

"Right," I said, peering at his rudimentary sketch of a girl with a wide hoop-skirted dress.

He pointed to the second figure. This one had a straight skirt. No belling out whatsoever.

"That's her," I said, leaning back in my chair. "I thought she must be wearing the latest fashion."

I'd been so focused on how pretty she was. How pretty her eyes were. That I hadn't even noticed just how different she really was dressed.

"Not the latest fashion," Graham said. Taking his piece of paper and dropping it into a desk drawer. "I'd bet money she's from the future."

"Son of a —" I sat back and gazed out the window at the

snow clouds hovering below us. The clouds were so thick, they looked like a person could walk right out onto them.

It was a far cry from Mississippi, where we had grown up.

I'd take the cold weather over the hot and hotter sweltering heat any day.

But at the moment, we had something far more important to worry about.

"Graham," I said. "There's something else you should know. Her name is Isabella Becquerel."

7

———

ISABELLA

The nap helped.

When I woke up, it was twilight.

Instead of a lamp on the nightstand, there was a candle burning in a little glass lantern.

The fire in the fireplace had burned down to nothing but glowing embers.

Using the pitcher, I poured myself a glass of water and walked across the room to one of the windows, taking the little glass lantern with me.

The rugged mountains peaks looked close enough to reach out and touch. And the clouds between here and there looked thick enough to walk across.

The sun splashed a rainbow of color across the snow-covered peaks as it set in the west.

I took my lantern and looked around the room a little more.

The only thing modern in the room was the running water.

There were no light switches or electrical outlets.

I didn't remember reading anything about the hotel being in its original state, so I had naturally expected modern conveniences.

I didn't remember hanging my wool coat in the wardrobe, but it was there.

The grandfather clock chimed the hour, echoing through the house.

Six chimes. Six o'clock.

I was pretty sure I hadn't had anything to eat since breakfast. A latte at the Denver airport before I got in the cab was about it.

After brushing my hair, I left the room and headed down to see what dinner looked like.

The halls and stairways were lit with candles.

There were paintings hanging everywhere. Mostly landscapes. Mountains. Rivers. Big horns and elk.

When I reached the first floor, things seemed to come to life.

I followed the sounds of voices and laughter to the dining room.

It looked like a regular dining room, not a restaurant like I had expected.

I stood at the door and watched for a moment.

My gaze was immediately drawn to Colton, but he didn't see me yet.

There were two couples sitting across from each other. And there was a baby, actually sitting quietly, in a high chair.

"We should take a railroad trip," one of the ladies said.

"You could do paintings."

"I think I'll just stay here," the other lady, obviously very pregnant said.

Colton saw me then. It was almost like he had been watching for me.

He jumped up and hurried toward me.

"There you are," he said as he neared me. "Are you feeling better?"

"Yes, I am, actually.

"Good," he said. "Are you ready to meet the family?"

"I guess," I said with a little smile. "Are there other guests?"

He didn't answer, just turned and introduced me to everyone looking this way

"These are my sisters Bailey and Dakota," he said. "And their husbands Graham Daniels and Zachary Rivers. And that's little Annabella."

"Hello," I said, not moving. "I'm sorry. I didn't mean to intrude onto your private family time."

"Nonsense," Bailey stood up and walked straight to me.

She was wearing a long dark gray dress that belled out around her. She had a lovely cameo at the center of her collar, adding to her sedate appearance. She looked like a southern belle from the movies.

"Please," she said. "We'd love to have you join us for dinner."

She took my hand and pulled me toward the table.

I glanced at Colton as I had no choice other than to follow. He just shrugged.

Bailey kept talking. "Colton said the elevation was bothering you. That happened to Dakota, too, when she first visited. But she lives here now and she's completely adjusted. It just takes a little time is all."

Colton was right behind us and held the chair where Bailey indicated that I should sit.

He sat in the chair next to me, across from where he had been sitting when I came in the room.

The Daniels and the Rivers families pulled me right into their fold.

As did Colton Auclair.

8

COLTON

I had initially been worried that my family would overwhelm Isabella, but she melded quite seamlessly into their fold.

Bailey was the social one in the family. She could talk to anyone. Even Dakota seemed taken with Isabella.

I knew that Graham wanted to talk to her and he studied her without being obvious.

He'd nearly fallen out of his chair when I'd told him her name.

Isabella Becquerel.

It wasn't Isabella that was disconcerting, it was Becquerel.

We all knew the story of Vaughn Dupre Becquerel. How her life was saved when an ancient Druid had cast a spell to save her life. A spell that sent her through time. A spell that she carried in her blood. That spell had been passed down through the generations.

It was how both Graham and Zachary had gotten here. And not just them, but the two men my other sisters had married, too.

That meant that somehow all four of my sisters had

married men from the future. Men who were somehow; albeit very distantly related to Vaughn Becquerel.

And now a woman named Isabella Becquerel had showed up on our doorstep.

This was not an accident.

I understood Graham's interest in talking to someone else from the future and as soon as he told Zachary, Zachary would want to talk to her also.

I was concerned for a different reason altogether.

I was a bit troubled because I found this girl, Isabella Becquerel intriguing. And it wasn't just because she might be from the future. I'd been smitten even before Graham had suggested that she might be from his time.

After dinner, we all retired to the parlor. Unlike traditional homes where the ladies retired with other ladies and the men went off to smoke cigars together, we all stayed together.

Graham didn't seem inclined to say anything to Isabella tonight.

"Since we have a guest," Bailey said, "we could play one of our parlor games."

"That's a good idea," Dakota said. "How about musical chairs? I can play the piano."

"We don't have enough people for that," Zachary said. "We need something for a smaller group."

"The story game," Graham said.

Everyone seemed to like that idea. And as far as I could tell, it seemed harmless enough.

"How does this work?" Isabella asked as Graham and Zachary arranged six chairs in a circle.

"Someone starts a story," Dakota said.

Graham brought over a little basket and put six pieces of paper inside. "Pick a number, he said. "That's the order we go in." He held it out to Isabella. "You get to pick first."

"Okay." Isabella reached in the basket and pulled out a scrap of paper. Looked at it. "Do I tell you?" she asked.

"You have to tell us," I said. "So we know who goes first."

"I'm number six," she said.

Everyone else quickly pulled their numbers.

I pulled number one.

This just might be interesting.

Since I was number one, I pulled a card from a stack of cards Bailey and Graham had put together. Each card had a different story starter sentence handwritten on it.

"Once upon a time, I…"

I looked around at the group.

Took a deep breath. "Once upon a time I found a beautiful girl standing alone on the side of the road."

Isabella looked away, but not before I saw the lovely smile that crossed her features.

9

ISABELLA

This was about as far away from how I expected my day to go as I could have imagined.

Playing parlor games with the owners of the hotel where I was supposed to meet Thomas. Thomas who had not shown up. With no cell phone service, I was unable to even text him.

The six of us sat in their parlor. A cozy fire going in the fireplace. The guys had a drink in their hands. The ladies did not. Apparently they were both pregnant. They offered me a drink, but I just took water.

The game as they explained it was to make up a story as a group. Each person got a turn starting the story off with one sentence and we had to go in the order we had drawn. Each person got to add one sentence to the story.

Colton, the guy who had rescued me from the side of the road went first.

"Once upon a time I found a beautiful girl standing alone on the side of the road."

His words made me smile, especially since he had been looking at me when he said his line.

Bailey went next. "Red birds and blue birds flew all around

her while chipmunks skittered at her feet."

Zachary. "When I rumbled up in my wagon, the birds and chipmunks all scattered, running for their lives."

"Thanks Zachary," Bailey said with an eye roll. He just grinned.

Dakota. "But they weren't running from me. They were running from a rain storm."

"That's two sentences," Zachary said.

"Maybe it's a semi-colon," Dakota said.

"It's okay," Graham said. "It's raining. My turn. Then the beautiful girl vanishes and no one knows where she went."

"Your turn," Dakota said, looking at me.

"You guys don't make this easy," I said. "Okay… She was a water nymph so when it started raining, she vanished into the mist only to come back when it stopped raining because she was a broken nymph who needed true love in order to become a true nymph again but it never happened because there was a bear who stole her trunks."

All five of them just looked at me.

"I think that's one of the longest sentences I've ever heard," Zachary said.

Then everyone was talking at once.

"What does that even mean?"

"I think we should give her some kind of prize."

I didn't know what it meant either. I'd never even played a game like this, so I didn't get the point to begin with.

"How many rules did I break?" I asked, leaning over toward Colton.

"I don't know," he said. "Probably all of them. But that's okay. It gives them something to talk about."

I bit my lip. "Sorry. It just sorta rolled out. Must be the elevation."

"I'm sure it is," he said. "Want to get some fresh air?"

"Sure," I said.

While everyone was talking and getting ready to play again, Colton and I ducked out and headed toward the back door, stopping at a cloak room.

"You can wear this," he said, putting a heavy cloak over my shoulders and fastening it at the neck. Then he put on the coat he had worn earlier.

He pulled a scarf off the coat rack and wrapped it around me.

"Are we going for a hike?" I asked.

"It gets cold fast," he said. "I can't have you catching your death."

I almost laughed, but caught myself as I realized he was serious.

He put on a scarf, too, then opened the door.

The cold wind slapped me in the face.

"You're right," I said. "It's amazingly cold."

"We're up really high in elevation," he said.

"I know."

We stepped out onto the back veranda and sat on a wooden swing that hung down from the balcony on one end.

"This isn't anything like I expected," I said, tucking my hands inside the warm fur-lined cloak.

"What did you expect?"

I expected to meet my boyfriend here. To try to convince him that we should go to Denver instead. And to try to hash out what we were going to do about our long-distance relationship.

"I don't know," I said.

"Do you mind talking to Graham?" he asked. "My brother-in-law?"

"No," I said, but a little shiver ran up and down the back of my neck. I didn't feel like I was in danger. Nothing like that.

But something was off.

Something was not as it should be.

10

COLTON

I gently rocked the swing with a foot as I sat side by side in the freezing cold next to Isabella.

Moonlight reflected off the snow-capped mountain peaks, giving them a shadowy mystical appearance.

It was almost surreal being here. With Isabella. Something felt so right about it.

In fact, nothing had ever felt so right.

But at the same time, I knew that she really wasn't supposed to be here. Unless…

"You said you came here to meet someone," I said.

"I was supposed to meet a friend," she said.

"A friend as in a beau?" I asked, holding my breath as I waited for the answer.

"A beau?"

"A husband?"

I did not want to know the answer, but I had to know. I had to know if she was married. If she was married, I was going to simply hurl myself off the side of the mountain.

"No," she said. "I'm not married."

I nodded, watching the fog from my breath as I slowly released it. "Good."

"Why good?" she asked, looking at me sideways.

"Just good," I said. "I think it's snowing in the valley below us."

"Really?" She looked over my shoulder. "How cool is that."

"It's really cool," I said, smiling to myself at the expression I'd heard Zachary say. "But I don't think you're going to be able to leave here anytime soon. The road gets slippery and impassable."

"I would think so," she said.

She didn't seem worried about being stuck here.

"Do they, your family, live here in the winter?" she asked.

"Of course."

"How do they stay warm?"

"Lots of fireplaces," I said.

"It must take a lot of firewood."

"It does," I said. "I did my share of chopping trees."

"You?" she asked with a little tone of surprise.

"Yes. Me. I do all sorts of things."

"Okay."

We sat quietly for a few minutes.

I was thinking it was time for us to go back inside before we froze to death.

"Is this some kind of immersive experience place?" she asked, shivering.

"What's an immersive experience?"

"You know," she said. "Immersing yourselves into the past."

"Come on," I said, standing up and holding out a hand. "I can hear your teeth chattering."

She put her hand in mine and together we went back inside the warm house, straight to the iron stove in the kitchen.

Once we started to warm up, I took off my coat and took her cloak.

I hung them back up in the cloak room, then went back to her side.

"We should probably stay inside now until the storm passes," I said, taking her hands and holding them between mine as she continued to warm up.

She laughed. "I think you're right."

Then she looked at me with those lovely green eyes that nearly took my breath away.

Between her eyes and those lips, I could hardly look away from her.

"So tell me," she said. "What kind of place is this exactly?"

11

ISABELLA

We sat in a little parlor with a fireplace, of course. All the rooms, it seemed, had one. They had to. It was the middle of summer and absolutely freezing. I couldn't imagine what it must be like in the dead of winter.

There was a painting on each wall. Bailey's paintings, I knew now.

I sat on a sofa next to Colton. Graham sat across from us in an armchair.

The parlor was surprisingly well lit with just candles.

I looked from one of them to the other.

"We don't mean to alarm you," Graham said. "But there's something you need to… consider."

"Okay," I said. "Should I be worried?"

"About us?" Colton asked. "No. You're safe with us."

"What is it then?" I asked.

I still couldn't quite get a grip on what kind of place this was.

Maybe I had fallen down a rabbit hole.

"Isabella," Graham said. "This is 1870."

I looked blankly at him for a moment.

"Right," I said with a little laugh. "I get it. I mean… I didn't know that's what this was. I just thought it was an old hotel."

Colton and Graham looked at each other.

"You don't understand," Graham said. "You're from the twenty-first century, right?"

"Right."

"So am I," Graham said. "But Colton and his sisters… they aren't. They're from this time. The 1800s."

"But… I don't—"

I couldn't figure out what he was trying to say. Why would some of them be from the past when the others weren't?

"Is this some kind of game?" I asked, with sudden inspiration. "One of those Escape Room games?"

I'd always wanted to do one of those. This could actually be fun.

"Not a game," Colton said.

Graham leaned forward, his hands clasped in front of him. "Isabella," he said, running a hand through his hair. "Have you ever done one of those games?"

"No," I said with a smile. "But they sound fun."

"No," he said, shaking his head. "You have traveled to the past."

"I don't think so. This is one of the clues, right?" I turned and smiled at Colton. "Why didn't you tell me?"

He shook his head and looked at Graham again.

"Let's give it some time," Graham said.

"Okay," Colton said.

"Have a good night," Graham said, leaving us alone.

"I think I must have offended him," I said, alone with Colton now.

"Graham isn't offended," Colton said. "He's just worried about you."

"He doesn't need to worry about me," I said.

"I'm worried about you, too," Colton said.

"I'm okay," I said. "I'll figure this thing out."

Colton ran a hand through his hair, much like Graham had done a few minutes ago and looked into my eyes. "You just don't understand," he said.

"Okay," I said. "You're right. I don't. Can you help me understand?"

Colton looked at me sideways. "How?" he asked. "How can I help you understand?"

I just shrugged. "You'll think of something."

12

———

COLTON

I paced back and forth in Graham's study.

Graham sat with a glass of whiskey in one hand, staring into space. The ladies had gone to bed, but we stayed up.

"She wants me to prove it to her," I said, reaching one side of the room and turning back.

Graham shook his head. "I don't think you can."

"But you did it," I said. "You convinced Bailey."

"That was different," he said. "First of all, I knew it before Bailey did. And second, Bailey had already seen her brother-in-law vanish."

I paced some more. "Isabella thinks we're playing some kind of game. Do you know what she's talking about?"

"Sort of. Maybe. I never played one of those locked room games."

"We have to think of something," I said, staring into the fire. I couldn't even begin to understand half of what Graham meant when he talked about the future.

"Actually," Graham said. "You don't."

"What do you mean?"

"I mean let her figure it out for herself."

"I don't have much choice, do I?" I asked, taking a sip of my own whiskey.

"Not really," Graham said. "But. There's something else I'm actually more concerned about."

"What's that?" I asked, dropping into the chair next to Graham's.

"You."

"Me?" I shook my head. "Why are you concerned about me?"

"Think about it," Graham said. "For some reason, all four of your sisters married men from the future. Men who carry Vaughn Becquerel's blood."

"I guess you were all in the right place at the right time."

"I don't believe that and neither do you," Graham said. Graham was slow to anger, but I heard an undertone of annoyance in his voice. "Do you think Bailey and I just happened to end up together? By being in the right place at the right time?"

"I don't know," I said. "How do you make sense of it?"

"I think there is some kind of connection." The anger had faded. "Something about the Auclairs. I don't know what it is and I might never know. But…"

Graham stood up. Leaned his forehead against the fireplace before turning around to face me again.

"But what?" I asked.

"Isabella is a Becquerel."

"I know," I said.

"That means she is a direct descendant of Vaughn."

"And she found me," I said, staring into the flames.

"That's right," he said. "She found you. Do you know what that means?"

"I think I know where you're going with this," I said. And I really didn't want him to tell me.

"I think the two of you are fated to be together."

"Nonsense," I said.

Graham stared me in the eyes. "Are you telling me you don't believe in fate? After four men from different parts of the country traveled to the past just to end up with your sisters right here in Whiskey Springs."

"I'm not saying that," I said. "I'm not saying I don't believe it."

What I was saying was that I didn't have to like it.

If he was right, it meant that I had no free will.

Well. I knew exactly what to do about that.

13

ISABELLA

I woke the next morning to the sound of birds. The birdhouse on the second floor of my condo attracted all sorts of birds. Red birds. Little wrens. Sometimes blue birds, but they ran the other birds off.

A typical summer day in Houston.

Except that it wasn't. It was cold. Too cold.

As I lay beneath the blankets, trying to convince myself to get up and turn up the air conditioning, I realized that I was not in my own apartment.

I was in Colorado at the Daniels House.

And there was still no electricity. The only light was from the early morning sunlight coming through the windows.

Reaching over to the nightstand, I grabbed my cell phone and lay on my back, staring at it.

It was blank.

Just blank. Like a black mirror of some sort. When I tried to turn it on, there was no power. The battery was completely drained on it.

I dropped it onto the bed. Worthless.

I leaned up on one elbow and looked around the room.

My suitcases were stacked next to the wardrobe. Someone had placed all my clothes inside the wardrobe, neatly sorted.

It was odd. Having someone unpack my things. It was also odd because I had only seen a couple of staff. I'd caught a glimpse of a cook and I'd seen a woman walking around carrying a basket of linens.

This really did seem more like a private home than a hotel.

Graham and Colton, Graham mostly, wanted me to believe that this was the past—1870—and I was from the future.

So from what he'd told me, Graham and Zachary... and me... were from the future while Bailey, Dakota, and Colton were all from the past.

Furthermore, Bailey, Dakota, and Colton were all siblings. That part I believed. They looked similar enough. The same dark hair. The same bright eyes with long, full lashes.

Their expressions were similar, too.

But Graham and Zachary were nothing alike.

How did I get put in the same category with them?

I picked up my phone again. And where was Thomas?

He had gotten me into this and he didn't even bother to show up.

I needed to find a phone. Or a computer. Surely they had one somewhere that I could use. Just for a few minutes. There had to be an emergency phone line.

If Thomas had stood me up on this trip, then I was going to just end the relationship.

I should have done it a long time ago. I'd known it wasn't going anywhere before he even left for San Francisco, but he kept me safe from the dating world. As long as I had Thomas, I didn't have to worry about dating.

That's what my therapist said, anyway. Made some sense to me.

As I got dressed, though, it wasn't Thomas that I was thinking about. It was Colton.

I stood at the wardrobe and contemplated my clothes. I had brought mostly casual clothes. Jeans and t-shirts. Sweatshirts. A couple of lightweight skirts. But I didn't have anything that would fit in with the other ladies here.

Bailey and Dakota wore long dresses. The closest thing I had was the skirt I'd worn yesterday.

Not wanting to wear the same thing I wore yesterday, I decided on jeans and laid out my clothes for the day.

I soon discovered that there was no hot water. Annoyed and not sure what to make of that, I took a spitbath and got dressed.

I did the best I could with my hair, finally just brushing it out and leaving it down.

Maybe the game hadn't started yet this morning.

Maybe they would let me use a phone. Even a land line would do. But there was a problem with that, too.

I had Thomas's phone number in my cell and since it had no battery whatsoever, I couldn't call him. Since his number was stored in my phone under his name, I didn't know his phone number.

As I walked down the first flight of stairs, I remembered that Thomas had made the reservations. They would have his number on file.

Feeling better, I started down the second set of stairs.

The grandfather clock chimed the hour. Eight o'clock.

It was later than I normally got up, but it seemed like I was the only one up this morning.

I went straight into the dining room and was greeted by the cook.

"Good morning," he said.

"Hi," I said.

"My name is Benson," he said. "Have a seat and I'll bring you some breakfast."

Not knowing what else to do, I sat at the table and waited.

Benson brought out a tray with coffee. The pieces were old-fashioned. Little matching bowls for sugar and cream.

No latte this morning, it seemed.

"Do you have a phone I can use?" I asked after Benson dropped off the coffee tray.

"No," he said. "My apologies." He poured coffee into a little mug. Set it in front of me.

"Where's the hotel desk?" I asked. "I have an urgent matter I need to attend to."

"Hotel desk?" He seemed genuinely perplexed by the question.

"Never mind," I said. "I'll ask Colton."

"Apologies, Miss. Mr. Colton is not available today."

I turned around in the chair, glancing out the window at the snow covered ground. "Not available? Where is he?"

"I'm not at liberty to say." Benson went back into the kitchen, leaving me there, alone, in the dining room.

I sipped the coffee, then added several spoonfuls of sugar and some cream. It was still going to be bad, but I knew that if I didn't drink it, I would have a headache before too much longer.

Benson brought out a plate with scrambled eggs, two biscuits, and bacon.

I contemplated not eating until I had answers. But my stomach growled and I caved. I was almost finished eating when Bailey came into the room.

"Good morning," she said.

"Hi." I forced a smile on my face. Bailey was dressed much as she had been last night. A sedate emerald green dress, again with a belled-out skirt. She sat across from me and arranged her skirts around her.

"I hope you slept well," she said as Benson brought her coffee and a plate.

"I did," I said. "Thank you."

I was feeling testy, but I had no reason to take it out on Bailey.

Nonetheless, I was a woman on a mission. "Do you have a phone I can use? I wouldn't ask, but my phone is out of battery and I need to find out why my friend isn't here."

"You'll have to talk to my husband about that," she said.

I nodded. "Okay." So that told me there was no break in this immersive experience. Apparently it never stopped. "Is he up yet?"

"He's not available today."

I looked out the window again. "How can he not be available? There's a storm outside."

She smiled. "He and Colton went fishing."

"Fishing? Seriously?"

"There was a break in the storm," she said. "They won't be gone long. They should be inside by lunch actually."

I pressed my fingertips against the corners of my eyes. "Okay," I said. "Is there a hotel desk where I can use a phone?"

She shook her head. "Again. You'll have to talk to Graham. Or maybe Zachary. Zachary should be out shortly."

"Sure," I said. "Thank you."

"After breakfast," she said. "We should find you something to wear."

"Something to…"

I looked down at my jeans. She was trying to get me indoctrinated into whatever was going on here.

I appreciated their hospitality, but I wasn't so sure about getting too involved.

"At least come look," Bailey said. "I want to show you something."

Bailey was so very charming, I couldn't refuse her simple request.

"Okay," I said. It wasn't like I had anything else to do.

14

COLTON

I hefted the stringer of fish over my shoulder and scrambled over a boulder back up to the snowy and somewhat icy trail.

Graham and I had hiked upstream to check his fish traps.

Both Bailey and Dakota preferred fish over just about anything else, so he kept a regular supply of trout.

I think Graham liked to come out in the snow just for the adventure of it. We wore heavy coats, gloves, and hats and wore boots that gripped the ice and snow.

"Have you thought any more about Isabella?" Graham asked as he joined me, with his own stringer of fish.

"Nothing to think about," I said.

"Is that so?" he asked. "Seems a little different from where I'm sitting."

"She's just passing through," I said. "Nothing for me to worry about. I'll give her a ride back into town when the weather clears. Pick up the supplies and that will be that."

Graham walked along beside me a few minutes in silence. A coyote howled in the distance.

Personally, I was thinking about heading back to Denver in

a couple of months. Getting my own place. All my sisters were married, so they didn't need me around.

And I wasn't much into country living. I'd had a taste of the city and decided that it was for me. I liked being around other people. I liked having things to do. Restaurants to go to. The theatre. The orchestra.

All those things were starting to come to Denver and Denver was close enough that I didn't have to be too far away from my family. I could visit when I wanted to. But it was time to start making a life for myself instead of just following along in their wake.

Besides I'd had just about enough of fables and legends to last me a lifetime.

And right behind that thought came an image of Isabella.

Damn it.

The woman had gotten under my skin.

"Let me know when you want to talk about her again," Graham said.

I just grumbled something incoherent.

We walked in silence the rest of the way back to the house.

When the house came into view with its several chimneys sending smoke into the air, my resolve faltered.

As much as I didn't want to care, I knew I wouldn't be able to stay away from Isabella.

I'd come with Graham today thinking that putting some distance between me and her would help, but it hadn't helped one bit.

I was smitten.

I didn't want my fate to already be decided. I wanted to have the free will to decide my own fate. To pick my own wife. Not to just have her show up and be expected to just fall into line.

It wasn't supposed to work that way.

Graham and I went in through the kitchen, shed our

winter garb, and dropped the fish off with Benson who would make quick work of them. He'd make some kind of trout dish for dinner that would rival that of any of the fanciest restaurants.

I grabbed one of the pails of water that was always heating on the stovetop and took it with me upstairs to my room.

The downstairs parlor, as I walked through, was empty and quiet.

Nothing but the soft ticking of the grandfather clock filling the silence.

I went straight into my room and freshened up. After putting on a clean pair of black pants and a white cotton button down shirt, I felt like a new man. Another sign, to me at least, that I was more suited for the city life than the rugged outdoors.

Refusing to go looking for Isabella, I went out on the balcony and smoked a cigar. The sun was warm, but the air was still cold.

After about ten minutes, I was ready to come back in.

I had some correspondence to take care of, so I went down the hallway toward the stairs.

That's when I heard ladies' laughter coming from Bailey and Graham's room.

I stopped right there in the hallway and listened.

I heard Bailey say something, then laughter. I couldn't tell if there were three women in there or two. But I was pretty sure I heard Isabella. I knew it was her because it didn't sound like either of my sisters.

I must have stood there for well onto a full minute, not quite knowing what it was that had me locked in place.

Then I pulled myself together and went on downstairs. What the women did was not my business. I reminded myself again that Isabella was merely passing through. Not for me to worry about.

Graham, in the main parlor, caught sight of me and motioned for me to join him.

"I brought down that sextant you wanted to see," he said.

"Oh good," I said, sitting in the chair next to him and picking up the brass instrument.

I knew Graham had one of these, but I thought he had forgotten I wanted to see it. Since I was spending the summer here, I thought it would be interesting to play around with getting the elevation of some of the mountains or maybe to measure distances to mountains around us.

Holding it up, l sighted it across the room toward the stairs.

And there she was. Right there in my sight.

Isabella.

Stopping on the stairs, she looked in my direction and smiled.

She looked different. Very different.

I slowly lowered the sextant, but already, my heart was beating about a thousand beats per minute.

Bailey and Dakota were in front of her, but that barely even registered with me.

All I saw was Isabella.

She was wearing a lovely light blue dress. And not just a dress. A ballgown. The skirt was made of about a thousand yards of material. The décolletage dipped low into a sweetheart neckline. She wore long white gloves that covered her elbows.

And her hair... her shiny brunette hair fell in long soft waves around her shoulders. Someone had woven a matching blue ribbon through her hair.

She was more beautiful than any princess.

And all my thoughts about having free will to choose my own woman completely vanished.

There had been no more than a gossamer web of it to start with, but what was left completely evaporated.

Fate or not, this was the girl I wanted.

15

———

ISABELLA

When I saw Colton across the room, drunken butterflies danced in my stomach.

Somewhere in the back of my mind, it registered that I had never had butterflies with Thomas. Thomas had merely been comfortable. Like a pair of boots a person grabbed on their way out every day. Not to compare my boyfriend with a pair of boots, but…

The grandfather clock ramped up and chimed two times.

When the sound was no more than an echo drifting through the house, I took another step down.

Bailey and Dakota were in front of me, but I hardly even saw them. I hardly noticed that Graham was sitting next to Colton.

All I saw was Colton. He was gazing at me with those lovely blue eyes that I couldn't pull away from. To keep it from tremblings, I pressed a hand against the smooth wooden banister.

When I'd acquiesced and went with Bailey to look at clothes, I had not been prepared for her closet. She had dozens of ballgowns like this one. And dozens of what she called riding habits which I came to learn meant that they had skirts that weren't as full. The less full skirts made it easier for a lady to ride a horse; hence riding habits.

Then there were what she called everyday dresses. Casual dresses compared to the ballgowns, but her everyday dresses were as fancy as any wedding dresses I had seen, just in much more lively colors.

As the morning progressed, she had, quite smoothly, convinced me to try on a couple of dresses. Then she had pulled this one out.

"This one," she had said after I had it on. "Wear this one tonight. It's magical."

It was impossible to resist her, especially when she had so very many beautiful dresses. So after putting the dress on, I'd twirled in front of her full-length mirror and fallen in love with it.

Now I had a good idea why Bailey wanted me to wear this dress tonight. She was a bit of a little matchmaker.

And from the way Colton was looking at me, I would agree that there was a magic in the air if not in the dress.

Cinderella.

But instead of evil stepsisters, I was in… the past.

Even if this wasn't really in the past, for all intents and purposes, it may as well be.

I had gotten nowhere with Bailey or her sister Dakota, so I had given up and just went along with them.

By the time I reached the bottom of the stairs, Colton was there waiting for me, holding out a hand.

"You look lovely," he said as I put my hand in his.

"Thank you," I said. "Not what I expected to do today."

"Sometimes we get things we aren't expecting." He tucked my hand into the crook of his elbow and we walked toward the dining room.

"Is this a special occasion?" I asked.

"Just an evening at the Daniel's House," he said.

"Is it like this every night?" The others followed along behind us, focusing mostly on Annabella and the new words she was learning.

"Pretty much. My sister likes three things in life. Painting and Fashion."

"You said three."

"Her husband and child."

"So four." I smiled. "They seem very happy," I said.

"It's hard to believe they were born centuries apart, isn't it?"

I blinked.

But before I could answer, Benson was there, bringing out a trout dish that he had prepared.

"Are these the fish you caught today?" I asked.

"Something like that," he said with a little grin.

I was in trouble for so many reasons.

First of all, I had a boyfriend. Of sorts.

Second, I lived in Texas. And another long-distance relationship was out the question for me.

And third, this family seemed to think that they were living in 1870.

They dressed like it. Lived like it.

They were probably more authentically 1870 than the people who had actually been alive that year.

16

COLTON

*B*enson had done miracles with the trout. Trout and potatoes. With some fresh vegetables.

I didn't ask where things came from. Graham, being from the future, had a lot of ideas and he had the money to implement a lot of them.

Like indoor plumbing. The thing he had not figured out how to do… yet… was to heat the water coming through the pipes. I predicted that one day he would.

He did these things just for himself and his family. He could probably make a fortune if sold his knowledge, but since he already had a fortune, he was able to just sit back and enjoy his days with his family.

Isabella, however, was quite astute and did ask the questions.

"This trout is wonderful," she said, taking a bite.

Then she leaned over to me and whispered. "Where did they get fresh vegetables?" she asked.

"They have an indoor garden," I said.

"Really? Where?"

"On the other side of the house."

"How do they keep the plants alive in the cold?"

"Good question," I said. "And you know, I really don't know. There's a fireplace and some flour bags and… you'd have to ask him."

"It's okay," she said. "I think I'll just enjoy it."

"That's what I do."

She looked over to my plate. "What's that?" she asked. "I didn't get one of those."

"What? This crusted potato?" I stabbed at one of the little cubes of potatoes in my plate and looked over at hers. "I think you already ate yours."

"No," she said. "I'm certain I didn't."

I held my fork with the bite of potato on it over to her mouth.

She slid it off with her lips and smiled at me with her eyes.

"Umm. I remember now. I did have one."

Oh my.

This girl was sexy as hell and she might be a little bit bold.

I had never thought to wonder what women in the future might be like.

With four sisters, some older, some younger, I thought I knew everything about women. They had given me an inside track on how women thought and what those thoughts were.

But this one was not like them.

Being from Texas, she had enough southern in her that I could relate, but the future in her was something altogether different.

Something I wanted to learn about.

Even if she had not been from the future, I still would have been captivated by her eyes… her smile… everything about her.

The future simply added some intrigue that drew me in like a siren drew the sailors onto the rocks.

I had my plans. Moving to Denver. Sowing my wild oats. But this girl was giving me different ideas entirely.

17

———

ISABELLA

After dinner, Dakota went to sit at the grand piano. Very pregnant, she moved slowly, but she had that pregnant woman's glow about her in spades.

Lightly touching the keys, she started playing, softly at first, then she picked up speed and gusto.

"Can I have this dance?" Colton asked out the blue as we went into the parlor to listen to Dakota's music.

"Oh," I said, glancing around. No one was dancing. Since Dakota was playing the piano, her husband poured himself a glass of whiskey and went to lean against the edge of the piano to watch her.

Bailey and Graham sat on a fur blanket in front of the fireplace with their daughter Annabella.

I was seeing an interesting parallel to the future. In the future, the television was the center of the house. Here, in this world, presumably the past, the fireplace was the feature.

"I don't really know how to dance," I said. I knew he had to be talking about waltzing. Any other kind of dancing would have been completely out of character.

I especially didn't know how to dance in a dress like this.

"You don't have to worry," he said. "Just hold onto me." He leaned forward and lowered his voice. "Besides," he said. "It's just us."

I smiled and tucked a strand of hair behind an ear.

"Okay," I said. "But promise me you won't laugh.

"I would never laugh at you," he said with sincerity.

I believed him.

So since I believed him, I let him twirl me around the parlor to the beat of Dakota's music.

And even though he seemed to think that no one was paying attention, Dakota livened her music for us.

I smiled and enjoyed myself entirely, but after a couple of rounds, I needed to rest.

"Can we take a break?" I asked.

"Of course," he said, immediately, leading me toward one of the sofas.

I put a hand on my waist. "Sorry," I said. "It's the elevation, I guess." Or perhaps it was the corset. It wasn't tight, but it was tighter than I was used to.

"I'm the one who should apologize," he said. "I should have remembered. I'll get you some water."

After he left to go into the kitchen, I focused on taking deep breaths.

Dakota continued to play the piano. Zachary was sitting on the bench with her now, their heads bent close together.

Bailey and Graham were laughing as they played with Annabella who had apparently just learned to say the word *Dadda*.

I seemed to have stumbled upon a place where couples were happily married.

I studied Zachary for a bit as I waited for Colton to bring me a glass of water.

I'd spent some time with Dakota and nothing indicated that she was anything other than from here—the past.

I watched Zachary for any sign that he might be from the future like me.

I saw nothing. Just a man in love with his wife.

As Colton came back and handed me a glass of water, I realized that I was beginning to think of myself as being from the future.

It was, of course, nonsense.

But being here... wearing this dress... Colton... all these things had me thinking that maybe it wasn't so much nonsense as it seemed.

And even if it was, maybe this was a place I wanted to be. A place I could belong.

I needed to keep myself grounded. I wasn't ready to fall into this world completely.

"You said you're just visiting," I said. "Where do you live?"

I was thinking that the more I could learn about Colton, the more the pieces would fall into place and the more I could understand what, exactly was going on with these people.

Besides, I wanted to know everything about this man I was crushing on.

18

COLTON

I kicked myself for pulling Isabella into a dance when I knew she'd been having elevation sickness.

With her being so beautiful, it was just easy to forget that she had not been feeling well.

"My family has a home in Whiskey Springs," I said. "But my sister recently got married and she's living there right now."

"Another happily married sister?" she asked, with a vague wave of her hand.

"I know," I said. "It's a little embarrassing. There's one in Denver, too."

I laughed. "How is it embarrassing? I think it's amazing."

"There's only one explanation," I said.

"What's that?"

"They're soul mates."

"Oh. Well," she said. "And you believe that your brothers-in-law came from the future."

"I have no doubt," I said.

"How can you be so sure?" I shifted the water glass from one hand to the other.

"For one thing, I've been around them enough to know."

"And you think I'm from the future?"

I leaned back. Studied her. She was stunningly beautiful in the dress, but there was something different about her.

"I think so," I said. "It's very possible."

"What makes you think so?" she persisted.

I reached out and touched a strand of her hair. "Your hair maybe." Beneath the lovely brunette, there were little tiny streaks of lighter brown hair.

"Highlights," she said.

"Highlights?" This was something new. It suddenly occurred to me that since I only knew men from the future, there must be a whole lot of things I didn't know about. Things men wouldn't talk about.

"Yes. I have highlights."

I leaned closer, looking at her hair. "How does that work?"

"You really don't know?"

I shook my head.

"My stylist... hair stylist takes little strands of hair and lightens them."

"Lightens them how?"

"I don't know," she said on a laugh. "Bleach I guess. Chemicals."

"Do men do this?" I glanced over at Graham. I'd never known him to have streaks in his hair.

"They do actually," she said. "Some of them. But not most of them. I doubt you would."

"Interesting," I said. "What else do you do in the future that men don't?"

"Makeup," she said after thinking for a minute. "I'm not wearing any right now. But we wear makeup on our faces."

"My sisters have done that," I said. Since she wasn't wearing any makeup, I didn't think that was anything that would make her look different at the moment.

Other than that," she said. "I don't know of anything that would be noticeable."

"There is something," he said. "I just haven't figured it out yet."

"I think I know what it is," she said.

"Please," I said. "Tell me."

"It's from being from a different culture. The future is different from this."

"You have hot water that comes through the pipes?"

"Yes," she said with a little smile. "But we have movies and music and computers and airplanes and so many things you can't even imagine."

"I've heard of some of those things," I said. "What's your favorite?"

"That's easy," she said. "But it's tied to all the other things. My cell phone."

I'd heard of that, too.

"How is it tied to other things?" I asked.

"I can watch movies on it and play music and read books. I can look up anything at all. Anything at all."

"I thought a phone was for talking to people."

"It is," she said. "But it's more than that."

"Do you think you can live without it?" I asked.

This was suddenly a very important question.

Each one of my brothers-in-law had chosen to be here. Each one of them had come here involuntarily at first—just as Isabella had. But then each of them had made a choice.

They had chosen to stay here, specifically to live out their lives with my sisters.

I wasn't saying I wanted her to stay here...

But the thought of her leaving made me a little bit queasy.

"I don't know," she said, taking a sip of her wine.

How was it she could give me such a vague answer? One that left me all the more curious.

I had not realized it, but I had really been asking her if she would be willing to give up everything she knew to stay here in the past.

I shook off the thought.

She had a boyfriend. Not that she had said it specifically, but she had admitted that she had been meeting a male friend here.

A lady wouldn't travel somewhere to meet a man she wasn't seeing. She wouldn't do it now and I seriously doubted she would do it in the future. Surely human nature had not changed all that much over time.

"Tell me how the culture is different," I said, circling back around to her earlier statement.

"I don't know," she said, glancing around. "People aren't as… happy."

"Seriously?" I asked. "Why not?"

She seemed to ponder this for a few minutes. "I think it's because there are too many distractions. Too many options. For example, people can go on their phones and look at pictures of hundreds of potential… mates."

"And you can talk to them?"

"Yeah," she said. "Absolutely. Right then."

"I can't even comprehend that."

"No," she said. "It's comprehendible."

I set my fork aside and took a sip of wine. I'd suddenly lost my appetite.

"But, you know," she said. "I'm not sure it's what it's all cracked up to be. I kinda prefer to meet someone the old-fashioned way."

"How's that?" I asked, looking into her eyes, feeling a little bit of hope at her words.

"You know," she said with a little shrug. "In person. By accident even."

I grinned. "I rather like the way that sounds, too."

I had no choice but to just go with it. I wasn't sure how much longer I could fight my attraction to this girl.

19

ISABELLA

"Just hold it like this," Dakota said, repositioning the embroidery hoop I held in my hands. The canvas was a plain piece of cloth with the rough outline of a butterfly sketched on it.

Dakota had used paint to outline the simple image of a butterfly on the canvas and my job was to just follow it using little stiches of thread.

"This is harder than it looks," I said.

Dakota laughed. "No. Just pick a color to start with." She waited.

"Pink," I said.

She showed me how to thread the needle. How to get started.

"Just do that for a while," she said. "All along this line."

I made the next stitch on my own, then peeked over at what Dakota was doing. Her fingers moved deftly as she worked a rather complicated pattern.

We sat on the fourth floor next to the fireplace in what had started out as Bailey's painting studio and quickly became a general family room.

Bailey sat next to one of the windows, painting something on a canvas of her own. I couldn't see her work from here, but she was concentrating. She held a little wooden pallet in her right hand with little dabs of different colored paints. It was a messy job. She'd obviously mixed the paints on her pallet to make her own colors and her apron was smeared with touches of most of them.

The men were outside chopping firewood. We heard them talking and laughing as they worked.

They all got along well together, it seemed.

As I sat, carefully stabbing the needle in the canvas, I felt at peace. More relaxed than I could remember feeling in a long time.

There were no phones to check. No television or radio in the background. Just the sound of men working outside. The steady ticking of the grandfather clock drifting up from the first floor, the gentle swoosh of Bailey's brush as she swept it over the canvas.

One of the men yelled. Then there was a commotion outside.

Bailey tossed her paint and brush aside and dashed out the door to the balcony.

Dakota and I looked at each other. We could hear her talking to the men, but couldn't understand what they were saying.

Dakota stood up, not an easy feat as swollen as she was.

She was only gone a minute before she came back in.

"What's wrong?" Dakota asked, her face pale.

"They're okay," Bailey said, her brow creased. "But the horses got out, so they're going off to round them up."

"The horses?" Dakota sat back down. "How did that happen?"

"I don't know," Bailey said. "But there's nothing we can do about it."

"I guess not," Dakota said. "They'll be gone for a while."

"Anything I can do?" I asked.

"Nothing any of us can do except to wait."

Benson came upstairs with a tray of muffins.

Bailey and Dakota didn't hesitate to take a snack break.

Bailey took two bites, though, and set hers aside.

"What's wrong?" Dakota asked.

"I'll be right back," Bailey said rushing toward the restroom.

"Is she okay?" I asked, picking up a warm, freshly cooked muffin.

"Morning sickness," Dakota said. "It's not just for mornings."

I smiled at the way she said it, then sat back to savor the muffin that I discovered had little blueberries in it.

Maybe later, they would show me the little indoor garden. I was super curious about it.

Bailey came back out and sat on the sofa, putting her feet up. "I'm just going to rest for a bit," she said.

"Do you want your muffin?" Dakota asked.

"I don't want anything to eat."

"Try not to worry too much," Dakota said. "They'll find the horses."

"I know," Bailey said. "At least it's warmer today."

Finished with my muffin, I went back to my needlepoint. I think I was getting the hang of it.

I noticed that Dakota was sitting very still, her fingers clasped in her lap.

I stopped what I was doing and looked up at her.

Bailey had her eyes closed and didn't notice.

"Dakota," I said. "Are you okay?"

She shook her head. "The baby…" she said with a look of shock.

Bailey sat up, slamming her feet on the floor.

"Wait," Bailey said. "No. Anna isn't here. Or Zachary." She looked at me.

I shook my head, my eyes wide.

Bailey got up. Paced to the window and back. She shoved her hair back with one hand, the other one on her hip.

"We need help," she said.

"We need Doc Avery," Dakota said before letting out a wail.

"We can't. We don't."

"Where is he?" I asked.

The both looked at me.

"In town. Whiskey Springs," Bailey said.

I stood up. "I'll go get him."

Dakota was shaking her head, but there were tears in her eyes.

"It's too far for you to walk. No horse."

"It's not that far," I said, my mind racing. "I just need to bundle up and I'll be okay. I'll get him and we'll come back."

20

ISABELLA

I'd never felt so alone in my life.

There was nothing out here on the trail but me.

I'd heard about women who went hiking alone. Across the country, even.

But not me. I wanted nothing to do with it. I wanted to get to town, get Doc Avery, and get back.

I had on a heavy fur-lined cloak, borrowed. Gloves, borrowed. And a warm wool scarf, borrowed.

The only thing, actually that I was wearing that belonged to me was my boots.

But it was okay. I would return them all by nightfall.

Doc Avery would have a wagon or a buggy or something to ride in. I could ride back with him.

Not paying attention, I nearly lost my footing as a foot landed on a slippery rock.

I would be back by tonight.

A chipmunk skittered across the path in front of me. I heard a wolf… or maybe just a dog… howling somewhere in the distance.

There could be bears. And all sorts of wild animals.

I had no weapon.

I had just bundled up and ran out the door like I was running to grab a coffee at the coffee shop.

But instead I was out here in the middle of nowhere, trusting that I could find my way and that I wouldn't be eaten by a bear or a wolf before I made it to Whiskey Springs.

I ignored the slight dizziness. I didn't have time for elevation sickness. Besides. I was walking downhill. I would get better as the elevation decreased.

I just had to focus on getting down the hill to town. Finding Doc Avery. And getting help for Dakota.

Blocking everything out except for my mission, I focused on the trail. Fortunately, I was wearing a riding habit, borrowed, so the skirts were fairly easily maneuvered.

I reached the spot in the road where Colton had picked me up. The *Carriage Stop*. Good. I was about halfway there.

Maybe it was just me, but the weather was remarkably warmer down here and the sun was out in full force.

There was no snow either. It was like I crossed through an invisible door and everything changed.

The road even changed. It was blacktop now. I shrugged off the cloak and looped it over an arm.

I walked for about ten minutes before I saw a car.

A car.

I knew there had been something wrong with my new friends. They didn't live in the past. They just lived *like* they were in the past. And they did a remarkably good job of it.

Now that I was getting close to town, I felt a little funny wearing the dress.

The passenger, a lady, in the car, stared at me as they drove past. She wore dark sunshades, but I could see the judgement in her expression.

Unfortunately, I did not blame her.

But it didn't matter.

Dakota may not truly be in the past, but she was truly having a baby. And there was no one there to help her, except for Bailey and being sick and pregnant herself, she was in no shape to help.

I stopped at the first place I came to.

It was a souvenir shop/convenience store that I remembered passing on the way up to the Daniels House. It seemed like forever ago.

I got some strange looks as I walked across the parking lot toward the doors, but I didn't have time for curiosity or judgment.

I walked right through the front door up to the desk. I had time to catch my breath while I waited in line for an older woman buying t-shirts to check out.

Shifting from one to the other, I considered trying to jump ahead in line. I had an emergency, after all, but since I was already drawing undue attention to myself, I decided to just wait a minute.

The man at the register was probably in his late fifties.

"Good afternoon," he said as the customer in front of me walked away with her bag. "A good day for a stroll on the boardwalk?"

"I need Doc Avery," I said, ignoring his attempt at humor.

"Doc Avery?" He scratched his head. "There was a Doc Avery that helped with the founding of Whiskey Springs. Hey." His smile broadened. "Is this one of those scavenger hunts?"

"No," I said. "There's a woman." I pointed the way I had come. "Having a baby. She needs a doctor."

"A baby," he said, scratching his chin. "Have someone drive her into town."

"She doesn't have a car," I said. "She's at the Daniels House."

"How did you get here?" he asked, not smiling anymore.

"I walked."

"All the way from the Daniels House?"

"Yes," I said. "Please. You have to help her.

"Come on," the man said, leading me over to a table and chairs. "Come over here and have a seat. I'll call the sheriff's office."

He pulled a little pad of paper and a pencil out of his front pocket. "But first, let me get some information so I'll know what to report. Let's start from the beginning."

21

———

ISABELLA

According to the clock on the wall behind me, I waited for two hours.

I didn't have my identification or my phone or anything.

I'd just run, literally, into town to fetch Doc Avery.

Instead, I was sitting at a little store. Waiting.

Waiting for the police to report back.

The man, his name was Walter, had called the sheriff's office and reported what I knew. That Dakota Rivers was at the Daniels House having a baby. No transportation.

Walter had taken pity on me and gave me a bottle of water.

Every single person who walked through the door, looked at me. I was the only one wearing a dress, much less a long formal dress.

I just ignored them. There was nothing else I could do.

Sitting back, I closed my eyes and replayed the last couple of days starting when Colton had picked me up at the Carriage Stop.

So much had happened. I had become part of the family. At least that's what it felt like.

Colton and his family had taken me in and made me feel welcome.

They had indoctrinated me into their way of life — living in 1870.

There were still things I couldn't explain. Like the running water and the fresh vegetables, if they were indeed in 1870.

I was convinced they *believed* they were in 1870. There was a name for this kind of shared delusion. Or maybe it was just a way of life they had chosen. I'd heard about those things, too.

If I had my cell, I would call Thomas. Or at least check my messages.

A few minutes after I finished off my water and came back from the restroom, a police car pulled up and a young male officer stepped out. He wore a hat that made him look more like a forest ranger than a policeman.

The policeman spoke in hushed tones to Walter, then came over to my table.

I braced myself. I had not seen an ambulance go up to the Daniels House.

I was worried about Dakota. About Bailey. About the men out looking for horses.

"Hello," the policeman said. "I'm Officer Hadley."

"Hello," I said, sitting forward in my chair. "Did you find Dakota?"

"I didn't find anyone up there who was expecting a baby."

"What do you mean? Dakota—"

Officer Hadley was shaking his head. "No one by that name. No one named Dakota."

"But—"

I glanced over at Walter, but he was busy with customers.

"I'm gonna need you to come down to the station," he said. "We'll do some paperwork. There's a social worker on the way in to talk with you."

"I don't need a social worker," I said. "I need to get back up to the Daniels House."

Officer Hadley was shaking his head again.

"Ma'am," he said. "Don't make me detain you."

"What? I didn't do anything wrong."

"Maybe not, but if you don't come with me, I'm going to have to put you under an M-1 hold."

"A what? What's that?"

"Can I see your identification?" he asked.

"I don't have it," I said, then took a deep breath, when I heard my own voice rising. "I told Walter this. I don't have anything. Not even my cell phone. I left everything up there. At the Daniels House."

Tears were welling in my eyes. But I was fighting them.

I hadn't done anything wrong. I had just been trying to help.

"I know," Officer Hadley said, softening his tone.

"At least tell me your name," Officer Hadley said.

"Isabella Becquerel."

Officer Hadley peered at me. Then looked down at my dress.

He opened his phone. Looked at something. Looked at me again.

"Someone's been trying to reach you," he said.

"Who?"

He wrote something on a piece of paper. Slid it over to me.

As I stared at the piece of paper, he stood up and made a call on his cell.

A couple of minutes later, he came back on sat down in front of me.

"They don't have anything there that belongs to you."

"But… I had a room. They checked?"

Officer Hadley just looked at me with something akin to pity. "No room in either of your names."

22

COLTON

"That's all of them," Graham said.

Zachary, Graham, and I all led horses behind us. It had been a long day. A really long day.

When we got home, we'd try to figure out how the horses got out of the stable so we could prevent it from happening again.

But right now, we just wanted to secure the horses, get inside, and get something to eat.

We'd darted off this morning, thinking we'd catch them before they got very far, but no… they had all run off like they had good sense. Fortunately, like the good horses they were, they stayed together.

"I always thought horses were smarter than this," Zachary said.

Zachary was from the city, so he didn't know a lot about outdoors which included horses. But he was learning and he loved my sister. That made him a good guy in my book.

We put the horses in their stalls, secured everything and between the three of us, we decided it would hold until morning.

Zachary kept looking toward the house.

"Something's not right," he said.

"You're just not used to being away from Dakota," Graham said. "I'm sure she's okay."

Zachary mumbled something incoherent. I was inclined to agree with him, but on the surface, everything looked normal. Smoke was coming out of a couple of fireplaces. It was almost dark, so it made sense that they would have already closed down some of the rooms for the night.

We had no more than stepped inside the back door than Benson's face told us that something was, indeed, wrong.

"What is it?" Graham asked.

"Dakota's baby," Benson said, but Zachary was already headed for the stairs.

Graham was right behind him.

I stopped to take off my coat and gloves. Dakota needed Zachary right now. Not me.

Benson put a hand on my shoulder.

"Colton," he said. "There's something else."

Dread coiled in my stomach as I waited for Benson to deliver whatever bad news he had.

"Isabella is… missing."

"Missing?" This was about as bad as anything I could have imagined.

"Missing, how?"

"She went for Doc Avery," Benson said.

"Good," I said. "Doc is here." But I knew that wasn't what he was about to tell me. I was trying to wrap my head around what he was telling me.

"No sir," Benson said. "She never returned."

I reached for my coat. Put it back on.

"Mr. Colton," he said. "You need something to eat before you go back out. It's almost dark."

I put my gloves back on. "Exactly," I said. "She can't survive out there by herself.

"I'll tell the others," he said. "But I'm going with you."

"You don't need to do that," I said, pausing at the door.

"Give me five minutes to run up and tell Graham." He was already headed out of the kitchen. "Grab a biscuit," he said over his shoulder.

He was right. I needed my strength.

But daylight was burning.

23

ISABELLA

Officer Hadley let me use his cell phone to call Thomas.

As I waited for him to pick up, I walked outside. Paced back and forth on the sidewalk.

It was almost dark. It was too late for me to walk back to the Daniels House. Maybe Officer Hadley would give me a ride.

Even as the thought occurred to me, I knew it wasn't going to happen. He thought I was insane. And if Dakota… and Colton really weren't there, then I wouldn't have any place to stay. I had no way to pay.

"Thomas," I said. "It's me."

"I've been trying to reach you," he said.

There was something in his voice that had me on alert.

"You aren't here," I said, cutting to the chase. I would have bet my life on it.

"No," he said. "I'm sorry."

It was funny. I had been planning to break up with Thomas, but it didn't help. Knowing he wasn't here—wasn't coming— was cutting me to the quick.

He had set all this up and now he wasn't coming. I couldn't help but wonder if he had planned this all along. Probably.

"Look," he said. "The room at the Daniels House is paid for. You go ahead and enjoy it for the week."

Thomas had never spoken to me like this. I'd heard this cold tone before, but never on me.

"What happened?" I asked.

I heard him take a deep breath. He knew what I was asking.

"Lisa."

Of course. Thomas and Lisa had had a brief fling before I came into the picture. He had always spoken fondly of her and I had always suspected he still carried a torch for her.

"I see," I said. And I did. But I couldn't talk to him right now. I couldn't talk past the lump in my throat if I had wanted to.

"Goodbye Thomas."

I hung up and walked back inside.

I told myself this was for the best.

This was what I had wanted anyway. It had been coming for a whole lot longer than I wanted to admit.

In all honesty, I should have broken up with him when he moved to San Francisco.

At least now I was free.

"Thank you, Officer Hadley," I said as I handed his phone back to him. "I wonder if I might ask you for a favor."

"Before I drive you up to the Daniels House," he said. "I'd like you to be checked out by a doctor."

"For what?"

"Consider it a compromise," he said. "You do that and I won't detain you."

"I need to go back. Look for my things myself."

"I understand," he said. "I'll drive you up there in the morning."

"I don't even have a credit card," I said, mostly to myself, picking up the cloak and scarf draped over the back of a chair.

"Consider it a gift from the town of Whiskey Springs. We'll put you up in the saloon for the night. You can take a hot bath."

"The saloon," I said. That was just about par for the course. For a day that had started out so well, it had gone downhill.

Now I had to spend the night in a saloon.

But all things considered, I wouldn't mind a hot bath.

24

COLTON

We didn't find her.

Benson and I went all the way to town and found no clues whatsoever to tell us what had happened to Isabella.

We even found Doc Alexander. He had not seen Isabella. No one in town had.

I didn't need any clues. I already knew.

By the time we made our way back, I had a brand-new nephew.

Graham's training as a park ranger continued to be of use and usually when it was least expected. Like now with his sister-in-law giving birth.

"Congratulations," I told Zachary, taking a cigar from him. But my heart wasn't in it and there was nothing I could do about that.

I knew that Isabella had gone back to her future.

Zachary knew it, too.

We stood outside in the dark cold night air and puffed cigars.

Graham came out and joined us. Added his congratulations to mine.

Then the conversation turned to Isabella.

"We'll go out tomorrow," Graham said. "Start searching."

"There's no need," I said. "I know what happened. She went to where I picked her up and went back through time."

"We know you're right," Zachary said. "But on the outside chance that something else happened to her, we're obligated to go look."

"I know," I said. "And I appreciate it."

"She'll come back, "Graham said, blowing an impressive sequence of smoke rings into the moonlight.

"Agreed," Zachary said.

"I wish I had your confidence," I said.

"You want her to come back, right?" Zachary asked.

"Of course he does," Graham said. "Did you see them together?"

"That's my point," Zachary said. "He doesn't think she'll be back because he wants her to come back."

I shook my head. "She won't come back," I said. "Simply because she doesn't know that she can. She doesn't… didn't… know she was in the past."

"She's smart," Graham said. "She'll figure it out."

"Maybe," I said. "I'm gonna try to sleep, at least a little. I'll head out again at first light."

I put out my cigar. "Again, Zachary. Congratulations."

As I went inside, I heard them talking. I knew they would help me look tomorrow. And I already knew that we would not find any sign of Isabella.

She had gone back to her life. She had a beau back there. It was right that she return to him. Just because I had four sisters who married men from the future, did not mean that I would marry a woman from the future.

Maybe I would just go ahead and start getting ready to head

to Denver. My sisters had their lives here. Zachary and Dakota would be building their own place soon unless Bailey could talk them into staying in the big house with her, which so far she had done a good job of.

Either way, I was a fifth wheel around here.

I had oats to sow anyway. It was just I had no taste for oats at the moment.

Finding Isabella's door cracked, I grabbed a candle from the sconce in the hallway and went inside.

Her trunks were there. Her bags.

I reached into her handbag and pulled out the little black mirror that they called a cell phone.

I turned it over in my hands a couple of times and pushed some buttons.

Some images showed up on it and then it instantly went blank.

Try as I might, I couldn't get it to light up again.

It was a gadget I didn't understand.

If for nothing else, I believed that she would try to return for her things.

According to what I had learned from my brothers-in-law, this little piece of glass they called a cell phone was very important to people from the future.

Still. I had to go out tomorrow and look for her. Just in case she was injured.

That would be a travesty for the ages. For me to not go look for her, thinking she had gone back through time, when she was lying there, bleeding out, needing me.

The thought made me sick to my stomach.

It almost made me rush right back out right now, in the dark, to look for her, but that was illogical.

I put her things back where I had found them and closed the door to her room.

Before going to bed, I needed to see my sister and meet the

newest member of our family.

I forced myself to tuck my heartbreak away as I stood at Dakota's door and knocked.

As least I thought I had tucked it away.

She took one look at me and she saw it.

"She'll come back, Colton," she said. "You have to trust in fate."

"I guess I'm not good with that. What are you going to name him?" I asked, purposely changing the subject.

"We don't know yet," she said. "We're waiting for inspiration."

Inspiration. Something we all seemed to be needing right about now.

25

ISABELLA

Officer Hadley was true to his word.

And the room at the saloon wasn't so bad. It was actually kind of nice in an historical kind of way.

And since I had developed a sudden, unexpected interest in things related to the old west, specifically 1870, I soaked in all the history I could.

He was also right about the hot bath.

I soaked until the water cooled then got out and put on a pair of sweatpants and t-shirt the town had also sprung for.

I folded the dress and laid it across a chair.

It was surreal knowing that I had believed I was in the past.

I'd always considered myself to be a practical person. It served me well in my jobs. My current job being the manager at a fairly large department store.

I was good at keeping employees satisfied and customers happy.

Problem solving. That was a priority on my resume. And I'd had no complaints.

Dressed. Hair dried. I headed downstairs toward the lively piano music to find something to eat.

As I walked down the stairs, I noticed something I had not noticed on the way up the stairs.

The landscape painting.

I recognized the style. I was no expert on art, but I stopped and examined the signature on the nearest one.

B. Auclair.

Bailey?

The painting was called Dragon's Blood and the sky behind the mountains was a crimson red. No doubt the color it was titled after.

I examined two more as I went down the stairs to the bottom floor. They were all similar. Besides the two landscapes, there was one of two big elks, ramming their horns together. It was so realistic I could almost hear their cries of agony and lust.

So my delusion was based on reality.

Or… had I brought my delusion here with me?

That was a possibility I was reluctant to consider.

I wasn't seeing the doctor until morning. There was nothing they could do anyway. Give me medication, but that would not solve my problem.

My problem being that I had lost my phone, my computer, and my handbag.

And on top of that, I could not stop thinking about Colton.

Colton. A man who was either from 1870 or who thought himself to be from 1870. Frankly, I could not quite say which one might actually be worse.

When I reached the main room, the restaurant, I saw that there were only a handful of people in the saloon.

I sat at an empty table near a window and looked out at the street. Cars traveled up and down the street. People, tourists mostly, walked along the sidewalks.

It was a good place for couples. Families. Not so much for a single person like me.

It had been so many years since I had been single, I still had a hard time thinking of myself that way. It shouldn't be so hard, though, considering it had been nearly a year since I had seen my boyfriend.

Not for the first time, I wondered how long Thomas had been planning this. Just how long he had been seeing Lisa again and just hadn't wanted to tell me.

My thoughts circled away from him right along what had become a natural pathway to Colton.

I'd only known Colton for a short amount of time and already I felt closer to him than I had ever felt to Thomas.

It was so odd.

A woman, dressed in a beautiful lavender brocade dress with black lace walked in my direction. A long jacket draped around the back, reaching the floor to join the ruffled ends of the skirt, some of which were tied up in a back bustle. A black lacy top covered the beautiful woman's skin to her neckline and matched the black exposed underskirt in the front. Her hands covered in black gloves, left no exposed skin other than her face.

She wore a little matching purple and black cap on top of her head.

The quintessentially western lady, probably in her thirties, dropped into the other little wooden chair at my table and smiled at me.

"Good evening," she said.

"Good evening," I echoed.

Another girl, this one wearing a short red skirt that actually looked like one a saloon girl in the movies would wear stopped at our table.

"What can I get you to drink?" she asked.

"Tea for me," the lady in purple said.

Then they both looked at me expectantly.

"Just water," I said.

The saloon girl left us alone.

The woman smiled. "You'll be wondering who I am," the woman in purple said.

"The manager?" I asked. Whoever she was, she left me feeling more than a little underdressed. Oddly enough, at this moment, I would have felt much more comfortable wearing the dress I had left upstairs.

The woman laughed. "If only it were that simple. I'm more like an advisor."

"An advisor?"

The saloon girl returned with our tea and water. "Here you are, Ms. Becquerel," she said.

"Thank you," we both answered, simultaneously.

I looked at the woman with some alarm. The saloon girl left us, not seeming to notice anything out of the ordinary.

The woman shrugged. "My name is Vaughn Becquerel," she said.

"Vaughn?" I did a mental run down of people in my family. I didn't come up with anyone by the name of Vaughn.

"What kind of advisor?" I asked, decided to circle back around since I didn't recognize her name.

"Time," Vaughn said.

I carefully set the water glass back down on the table.

"A time advisor?" I asked, looking at her questioningly.

She sipped her tea, holding the little mug gently in both her gloved hands. Nodded.

"Is that like a life coach?" I asked. But even as I asked, I had the feeling that this was something else entirely.

"Yes," she said. "I suppose you could say that."

A time advisor whose name was Vaughn Becquerel.

I think perhaps seeing that doctor tomorrow wasn't such a bad idea after all.

26

COLTON

I sat on my favorite horse, the one named Lightning, so named for the little white bolt of lightning on his forehead. The only white on an otherwise black horse.

I sat at the end of Graham's long road, facing the Carriage Stop. A gentle breeze, carrying the scent of spruce trees, teased at my cloak.

The sun would soon be setting after a perfectly nice, sunny day.

Winter, it seemed, had finally backed away to allow warmer weather to fill the days.

Zachary and Graham had gone back to the house hours ago, both weary and ready to see their wives.

I wasn't ready to go back to the house. Not just yet.

I straightened in the saddle and watched the play of colors of the sunset reflecting off the mountains across the valley.

I'd planned on bringing Graham's sextant out here to measure their elevation and maybe try to figure out how far away the other mountains were from here.

But that had not happened yet. First, a late spring snow

storm had interrupted everything and then Isabella had breezed into my life only to vanish right back out.

Everyone. Graham and Zachary—men from the future. Bailey and Dakota—my sisters who loved them, insisted that she would find her way back.

I didn't think so.

Isabella had not really understood at a visceral level that she was in the past.

And why would she give up everything—her way of life and her beau—to come to the past to be with a man she had only just met?

Things did not add up.

And I done the math.

Still. I watched the path that led down the hill to Whiskey Springs. Tried to make sense of how she had ended up here to begin with.

She'd come to meet someone. Her beau. He, of course, would have gone to the Daniels House in the future while Isabella came to the Daniels House in the past.

Zachary had not stayed around to actually see it, but he believed that the Daniels House had two very different meanings in the past and the future.

In the past, it was just that. Graham Daniels's house. In the future it was the Daniel House Hotel.

Zachary had actually originally come to the Daniels House —in the future—in order to convince the owners—Zachary's descendants—to sell to an investment company that wanted it for hotel property.

The whole thing, in my opinion was far too much to fathom.

And to be honest, I hadn't paid it much heed until Isabella had appeared in my life.

Now I wanted to know everything. I wanted to know how the whole time travel thing worked. But apparently there was no science behind it. At least not one that anyone could figure out.

It was something that just happened.

The love spell running through Vaughn Becquerel's blood was better than any Cupid's arrow at getting people together, and not just together, but together across the boundaries of time.

It was nothing that any of us could figure out.

If Isabella was indeed my soulmate, then my family was right.

She would be back. Unfortunately, I wasn't sure I had the constitution to wait patiently for her.

I didn't see how I could win. If I waited, I ran the risk of her not returning. Then I would have missed out on finding the person I was supposed to be with.

Since I couldn't sit here all day and it was going to be getting dark soon, I turned Lightning around and together we headed toward the Daniels House.

I had a lot of things to think about. And as far as I could tell, there was no easy and perhaps not even a right answer.

It was one of those things where we simply had to do the best we could with what we knew.

Which was very little.

27

ISABELLA

"Do you love him?" Vaughn asked.

I looked into her eyes. Lovely green eyes, so deep and knowing it was almost painful to look into them. And in some ways it was almost like looking into a mirror.

Piano music swirled around us. The original piano, they said, from the 1860s.

"You're asking me about Colton?" I asked, knowing that she was.

"Who else would I be asking about?" she asked.

I shook my head and lowered my gaze. "No one."

"You have to give up this way of life," she said, with a quick glance around.

"I don't care about that," I said, a little surprised by my own answer.

I hadn't already come to that conclusion, had I?

Maybe I had and I just hadn't admitted it to myself.

"Alright," Vaughn put a hand over mine. With her gentle touch, I felt a calmness settle over me.

She was not the normal person. I could tell by her touch.

"I really was there?" I asked. "In the past?"

"Yes," she said. "You really were there."

I nodded and took a deep breath.

"I thought so." I glanced over my shoulder at the cars traveling up and down the street. So modern. So hopelessly modern. "Can I get back there?" I asked.

"You're certain that's what you want to do?"

"I am." I straightened in my chair. "What do I need to do?"

"First," she said. "I want to show you something."

"Okay. What is it?"

Vaughn reached in her handbag and pulled out a book—an oversized colorful book that looked like one of those coffee table books that no one ever opened.

But she did open it. Then she turned it around, seeming to remember to show me the cover.

The Auclair Family: A Pictorial History

"The Auclairs," I said, leaning forward.

"Yes," Vaughn said. "I haven't figured out how the Auclair family fits in with the Becquerels," she said. "You see, I'm your great great… great great grandmother."

"You're not that old," I said, brushing it off. "An aunt, maybe."

She put a hand over mine again. "Thank you. But I was born in the 1700s."

I leaned my head to the side as I studied her. "I hope I carry your genes," I said.

Vaughn laughed. "I like you."

I smiled.

"Anyway, I have a feeling that you have some doubts."

"No, I—"

"It's okay," Vaughn said. "You should question things."

She opened the book and laid it out flat in front of me.

Leaning forward, I looked at a large family photograph.

They were all there. Bailey, Dakota, two sisters I had not met… and Colton.

I lightly touched his photograph. "It's Colton," I said. leaning forward so I could see him better.

When I looked up at Vaughn, my eyes were moist. "It's true," I said.

Vaughn smiled. "Yes."

There were other pictures. Graham and Zachary were there, standing outside the house.

There were a lot of children. I took a minute to read the caption.

While she waited, Vaughn ordered wine.

"They had five children each?"

"Rather prolific."

"Colton never married?" I asked.

"This is where it gets complicated," she said. "In this timeline, after he met you, he never married."

"That means…" It meant I never went back to him.

The saloon girl brought over two glasses of wine. "Enjoy," she said.

"No," Vaughn said, seeming to read my mind. "This is what happens if you don't. If you do go back in time again, the book will be rewritten."

"How do you know this?" I asked.

"I've been around a few hundred years," she said with a little smile. "Actually, I've seen it happen over and over."

"Part of your time advisory job?"

"Yes. If you want to return to the past, to be with Colton, I can advise you on how to do that."

"You have a most interesting job," I said.

"Yes, I do," she said. "I just sort of fell into it."

I looked at her with questions.

"You don't know the story?" she asked.

I shook my head.

"They didn't tell you."

"What story?"

Vaughn took a sip of her wine.

"A long, long time ago, in a place far away." She stopped. Looked at me. "I lived with some very nice ladies in a convent. Sometimes I still miss them. Anyway, I thought I was going to grow up to be a nun like them, but they saw something else in me. They decided that I needed to marry. I was only fifteen."

"Why were you living in a convent?"

"My parents were killed in an accident when I was but a child. Since I had no other relatives and no one knew what else to do with me, they sent me to live in the convent. It was actually a very nice place to grow up."

"But they… had you get married?" The red wine was sweet and quickly dulled some of my anxiety.

"Not exactly. They sent me to America to marry a man who was in need of a wife."

"Right," I said. "1700s."

"Exactly. I made it to America and traveled up the Mississippi River. Once we were on land near Natchez, we were attacked by hostile Indians."

I sat quietly. Waiting for Vaughn to tell her story.

"They killed everyone." Her eyes met mine. "I was the only survivor."

"How?" I asked, knowing this had something to do with what she was trying to tell me.

"A man, an old Druid, asked me if I wanted to live."

"Of course you did," I said.

"He chanted and yelled at the heavens, creating quite a terrible storm."

"A thunderstorm?"

"Yes. He created a rip in time. I fell right through it into the 1800s."

"He warned me that those of my blood would also carry the spell in their blood." She looked at me. "That means you."

"I have a spell in my blood?"

"So it seems. And the rip never healed. I don't think it ever will. My daughter, Anna, has studied it. She's the one who sends me wherever I need to go."

"But… you're not related to the Auclairs."

"That part is a little murky. All four of the sisters have married men from the future. And the brother, it seems, is going to marry a woman from the future."

"You can't explain that?" I asked, ignoring the comment about Colton for the moment.

"Not even a little bit," she said.

I nodded. "It's fate."

Vaughn pushed her empty glass aside. "So now that you know how we got here, do you still want me to help you?"

28

___

COLTON

"**A**re you sure we can't talk you into staying for just a little bit longer?" Bailey asked.

"I don't think so."

"You could at least stay until the end of summer like you planned." Dakota swayed the infant in her arms and pouted.

The five of us stood in the parlor, saying our goodbyes.

It was early in the morning. Earlier than any of us would normally be up, but I wanted to get a head start into Denver. It was a long ride and I wanted to be there before dark. I normally would have stopped by Elise's home in Whiskey Springs, but I had just seen her less than two weeks ago. Recently married, she did not need her brother hanging around getting in the way.

Besides, it was time for me to make my own way. I'd always stood in the background, taking care of my sisters when they needed me, but now that they were all married, my work was done.

It was time for me to figure out who I was.

So my horse was saddled. I was a light traveler. One of the benefits of being a single man.

"We understand," Graham said.

Both Graham and Zachary had doubtless grown weary of trying to convince me that Isabella would be back. I obviously wasn't listening, so they stopped talking.

I hugged everybody.

Dakota, though she acted angriest, was the one who had tears spilling down her cheeks as I walked out the door.

Early morning mist still covered the ground.

My favorite part of the day. Everything was fresh and clean and the day held endless possibilities.

I mounted Lightning and took off down the path leading into town. I'd breeze through Whiskey Springs and keep going all the way to Denver.

From there I didn't know what I would do, but whatever it was, I would figure it out.

After reaching the Carriage Stop in short order, I stopped and allowed myself a few minutes of hesitation.

There was a possibility that my family was right. That Isabella could come back. But I pressed forward, moving past the spot where I had picked her up before and kept going.

Reaching into my pocket, I pulled out the little piece of glass that belonged to her.

Her cell phone.

It had lit up for me before. And having it made me feel closer to her.

If she came back, I would return it. I was simply keeping it safe for her.

At least that's what I told myself.

The other side of that coin was I needed something that was hers to hold onto.

It somehow made it a little bit easier to walk away.

As I traveled down the path leading to town, I fought against the urge to turn around. To go back.

To wait for her.

I could not explain my need to leave here.

And I could not explain the way my heart broke into a million little shards as I headed down the path toward Whiskey Springs.

29

ISABELLA

Vaughn was a very thorough time advisor.

If it hadn't been for her, I would have simply put my dress back on and raced up the path to the Carriage Stop and jumped right back in time.

But she had done this before. She instructed me to do what she called getting my affairs in order.

"You'll need money," she said.

First of all, getting my driver's license and credit cards replaced was such a crazy hassle, I had not even bothered to get my phone replaced. Besides, I couldn't see why I would need it when it wasn't going to work in the past anyway.

As I cashed in my retirement for the purposes of buying gold bars, the bank president had questioned me to the point that I started to get uncomfortable. He wanted to know if someone was coercing me to take my money out of the bank.

He urged me to contact the authorities to make sure I wasn't being scammed.

I had to admit, it did feel a bit like a scam, but the gold bars were not going to leave my hands. It wasn't like Vaughn was asking me for any kind of money.

On the contrary, she had said goodbye and told me that I would not see her again.

That made me a little sad. She was an exceptionally likeable woman that I would have liked to have called a friend.

Once I had everything together and was dressed and ready, I decided the best way to go about this was to recreate what I had done last week.

I took a cab up to the Carriage Stop, paid the driver in cash, and stepped out.

"Are you sure you want me to leave you out here by yourself?" This particular cab driver was kind and genuinely concerned.

He was probably also a bit concerned since I was wearing a long ballgown. Not the typical dress for a hiking trip in the mountains.

"I'll be okay," I said before I closed the door. "Really. But thank you."

Carrying my backpack with me, I went over to stand at the Carriage Stop.

The cab driver didn't leave right away. Probably didn't want the liability for me on his watch.

I held up a hand and waved at him.

He shook his head, but slowly drove off, no doubt despite his better judgement.

I waited. No luggage this time. Just the belt around my waist that held the four little gold bars that I had bought after cashing out my retirement.

That had been Vaughn's idea.

I watched the path looking toward the Daniels House. The seconds ticked past.

The bank president's words came back to me, as much as I didn't want them to.

Now my imagination was running a little bit wild.

It would be so easy for this to be a scam. The Auclairs and

their family could be running a ring of thieves. First they convince unsuspecting people that they are visiting the past. Make them want to come back. To live in the past.

Then they send in Vaughn Becquerel or someone with the same last name as the victim. Vaughn convinces the victim to cash in their life's savings to buy gold bars.

They would know that I—said victim—would have the gold on me. And since gold was not traceable, they could ambush me and no one would be the wiser.

Wealthy victims would be far more profitable than people like me. A girl with a string of student loans. Not much in savings. Maybe I slipped through the cracks. They could have been after Thomas instead, but if Thomas was wealthy I didn't know it.

Well, at any rate, what they did not know, was what I had in my pocket.

I carried a little pistol. It wasn't much, but it would take down an unsuspecting thief if I could get close enough to him… or her.

That bank president had gotten into my head almost as much as Vaughn had. Of course, I was a product of my environment and people these days, if they did more than a grab and go, were quite inventive in their scams.

One thing I did know. Dakota had been genuinely pregnant. That one would be hard to replicate.

I wrapped my fingers around the gun in my pocket and waited. Watching until my eyes hurt from straining.

I stood there about thirty minutes.

This was not working.

I had a choice at this point.

I could either go back the way I had come and pick up my life where I had left off. Since I was still on vacation, I had a job to return to. And time to get my cell phone replaced before going back to work.

Or… I could walk right up to the Daniels House.

They would probably be mad at me for not coming back with Doc Avery, but that had not been my fault. I had given that task everything I knew to give it.

I had certainly acted on good faith.

If they turned me away, again, I could just go back down this road to Whiskey Springs and hop on an airplane.

I could sell the gold to the next person who wanted the adventure of time traveling to the Auclair House.

The warm sun beating down on my head was cooled by a soft mountain breeze. Crickets chirped and chipmunks skittered. A blue bird landed at my feet and gave me a dirty look when I didn't toss him a peanut.

"You know the rules" I said. "No feeding the wildlife."

Without a word, he flew off. I huffed out a breath. He'd known he was in the wrong.

I waited a little bit longer.

Maybe I would just take a little walk up to the hotel.

See if I could see anything going on. Maybe catch them off-guard while they weren't expecting me.

Deciding that was an excellent idea, I headed up the path.

Uphill was decidedly harder than going downhill.

I had on good boots. Since no one was going to see my shoes, I opted to invest in a good pair of boots. They would last me forever and no one had to be the wiser.

Reaching a bend in the path, I saw an elk twitching his ears as he watched me out of the corner of his eye.

I stood very still, not wanting to startle him.

He must have finally decided I was not threat. He walked across the path and disappeared into the trees.

Appreciating the unexpected rest, I kept going.

The path was a bit muddy here, with little patches of snow that had yet to melt.

A couple of minutes later, I saw the house up ahead. It was

absolutely stunning. And it looked so different than it had during the winter storm.

Yet smoke still billowed out of the many chimneys. I'm surprised this house wasn't known for having an abundance of chimneys. Or maybe it was just a site to see with smoke coming out of all of them.

Since I was coming in from the side of the house, I decided to walk around to the back first.

And what I saw was an idyllic scene.

Bailey sat on a little stool, a paint canvas in front of her. Her husband, Graham sat on a blanket with their child, Annabella crawling over him.

I didn't see Dakota.

My heart skipped a beat as I realized that I would blame myself if something had happened to her during the birth of her baby.

I knew just enough about history to know that a lot of women died during childbirth.

The thought had me frozen in place. If something had happened to Dakota, I was the last person Bailey would want to see.

She would think I had failed her.

Then I saw a movement on the back porch.

With a sigh of relief, I saw Dakota coming out the back door, Zachary behind her, holding their baby.

Thank goodness. Everything had gone well with her and the baby.

With a smile of relief on my face, I walked toward the back of the house.

Zachary saw me first. He leaned close to Dakota and said something. Then they were both looking at me. Just standing there. Watching me as I came forward.

Then Bailey and Graham were looking at me, too.

I didn't see Colton anywhere.

And they weren't smiling.

I did not understand. I had unintentionally abandoned Dakota in her time of need, but she was obviously okay.

They had to know it wasn't my fault.

I stopped about three yards from Bailey and looked at her questioningly.

Something was wrong.

Very wrong.

30

COLTON

I sat in a rowdy saloon called the Salty Dog in downtown Denver.

A scantily clad woman played the piano. Although she played with obvious gusto, I could not help but compare her ability to my sister, Dakota.

Dakota rarely hit a wrong note, but this girl had discordance down to a science.

No one in the crowded saloon seemed to notice or care. All in all, it was even hard to hear the music over the talking and laughter.

Cigar smoke was heavy and smelled like liquor.

Several tables were crowded with men playing a game of cards, each man with a scantily clad woman standing… or sitting… at his arm.

The whiskey, flowing freely, tasted weak to me. I could not help but notice that this was in contrast to my first glass with strong whiskey.

All in all, the whole thing seemed quite suspicious to me.

But everyone said this was the place to go.

If the crowd was any indication, there was no question that they were right.

"Hello," a pretty young lady, also scantily dressed, leaving little to the imagination, approached me where I stood at the edge of the bar taking everything in.

"Hello," I said.

The young lady smiled and leaned forward to give me a better view of her assets. Her eyes were lined with coal and her lips unnaturally red, but underneath it all, she was pretty.

"My name's Charlotte," she said with a thick southern drawl. "But I'm not from Charlotte."

"Then where are you from Charlotte?" I asked.

"I'm from Atlanta."

"What are you doing all the way out here, Charlotte, not from Charlotte?" I asked. And do your parents know what exactly you're doing way out here?

Batting her eyes, she leaned forward and lowered her voice so that I had to strain to hear her. "I came west for adventure," she said. "Would you like to buy me a drink?"

I might be new to the city, but I had been to my share of bars. I knew how this worked.

"You can have mine," I said, handing it to her. "I'm not going to drink it."

She sniffed and shook her head. "I can't," she said. "It's against house rules to drink from a man's glass."

Of course it was. A man's drink contained alcohol whereas a lady's drink contained tea. The lady's job was to get the men to buy them drinks. The ladies would remain sober while the men continued to drink and to buy "drinks" for the ladies. It was a profitable game for the house.

Since I happened to be friends with the owner of the Whiskey Springs Saloon, I had been warned about these little tricks. Not that they were ever used at the Whiskey Springs Saloon.

"I think I'll pass," I said.

The girl pouted prettily.

There had been a time when I would have bought the lady a drink just so I could spend time with her. To have someone to talk to, no matter the topic.

But tonight, the thought of having to entertain any young lady, save for one, twisted my stomach into knots.

I had all but forced myself to come all the way to Denver. Had forced myself to frequent the popular saloons.

But I found my thoughts filled with a girl who shouldn't be. A girl from the future.

Isabella Becquerel.

I had come for the adventure.

But I was leaving for the girl.

31

ISABELLA

"**Y**ou're getting so much better at that," Dakota said.

I stopped. Held up my sampler and examined my precisely straight little stitches. I was inclined to agree with her.

"I have a good teacher," I said.

Dakota and I sat in front of the fireplace on the fourth floor of the Daniels House. Dakota rocked her baby while I worked on my needlepoint.

Bailey sat in front of an easel, swiping bold colors of paint onto a canvas. She was truly one of the most driven people I had ever met.

She spent several hours every day with either a paintbrush or a charcoal pencil in her hand. Most every day she produced a new piece of work.

It explained why her paintings had survived over the centuries. She was nothing if not prolific. It seemed that she who produced the most work survived the longest through time.

Bailey was most impressive.

It had been five days since I had walked back through time.

I had known something was wrong the minute I saw their faces.

I soon learned that Colton had left for Denver earlier than he had planned.

According to all reports, Colton had looked for me for days. All the men, even Benson, had looked for me, but Colton had been the last to give up.

After I didn't come back, he had gone a little mad. Walking the halls. Staring from the windows for hours.

Finally, unable to go on like that any longer, he had saddled up his horse and rode off. On his way to Denver.

Dakota and Madison said he had planned on leaving for Denver at the end of the summer. To find a place for himself there.

But he had gone early.

They had all offered to write him, but I had urged them not to. I did not want him to feel like he had to come back here for me.

I had almost left to go back to the future.

The girls had asked me to stay awhile.

They both insisted that I had not traveled back in time for nothing.

There had to be a reason.

I believed there was a reason, but my reason had gone to Denver.

And I was not so presumptuous to believe that I could follow him. Even if I wanted to.

Since I enjoyed their company and because I had blown up my life in the future. All my money was now in gold bars I wore in a belt around my waist. I no longer had a job. I had nothing.

So I decided to stay for a while. To soak up some culture of the old west.

It was quite the honor to be here in person.

There was one little, minor problem.

If I wanted to stay here in the past, I couldn't travel the road that led to Whiskey Springs. Somewhere in there—the Carriage Stop—it seemed, was my portal to the future.

I had not figured out the implications for that and Vaughn had not said anything about it.

So I stayed here, waiting for inspiration. Enjoying the peacefulness that came from living in a castle on top of a mountain.

And deep down... maybe not so very deep... I secretly... maybe not so secretly... wished for Colton to come back.

32

COLTON

I made it a week. A whole week.

It was all I could take.

I had learned something very valuable. Very quickly.

Denver was not for me.

I would have sworn it was going to be. My sister Andrea lived in Denver, but she and I had never really been that close.

The one night I had spent at her house, I had felt like a fish out of water.

She had two little ones now and the whole family, all four of them, lived in a small house with very little privacy.

My perception admittedly was colored by having just come from Graham and Bailey's monstrously huge four-story house. A house so big it was hard to even keep up with where everyone was at any given time.

So on a bright Wednesday morning, I saddled up Lightning and we went west.

I had not felt this chipper since… since that morning before Isabella had vanished. Even out looking for the horses, just knowing she was at home waiting for me had given me joy.

Then the rug had been jerked out from under me.

I'd tried to put her behind me. I'd tried not to think about her. To just move on.

But I soon learned that it did not work that way.

One did not just put the love of his life out of his mind and move on like nothing had happened.

A lesson learned. A heard lesson learned.

I rode all day long. But it was a clear day—perfect weather—and Lightning didn't mind any more than I did.

We went right through Whiskey Springs, not even stopping for a break.

Instead of going straight up to the house, though, I decided to follow the river road and come up the back. I normally didn't go that way. It was more scenic, but took a tad bit longer. It was worth it.

The setting sun dropped behind the mountains splashing rays of gold behind the clouds and reflecting pinks and golds in the snow below.

It was beautiful.

I wish Bailey could see this spectacular sunset so she could put it on a canvas.

The little black glass mirror device—cell phone—vibrated in my front coat pocket.

I nudged Lightning to a stop and pulled out the device.

Holding the phone up, I looked at the sunset through it, centering it just right. Like I imagined it would look in a painting.

Sort of like one would use a sextant.

Wanting to get to Graham's house before dark, I put the phone away and nudged Lightning forward.

I wasn't surprised that the phone had come to life for me.

I actually took it as a good sign that I was doing the right thing by going back to my sister's house where I had spent time with Isabella.

And as I rode toward the setting sun, I dared to believe that Isabella just might be there waiting for me.

There was nothing wrong with wishing.

Nothing wrong with a little magic.

And nothing wrong with wishing for a little magic.

33

ISABELLA

It was such a beautiful evening that I decided I would take a walk.

I loved the Auclair sisters and their husbands, but sometimes, I just needed to get away. To have a few minutes off by myself.

I wouldn't go far, of course, but it felt good to stretch my legs. To get outside and breathe some fresh air.

I walked along the river, never toward the Carriage Stop.

Just as I reached what they called the Whiskey Springs waterfall, I stopped and looked back the way I had come—west.

The setting sun splashed an array of pink and gold colors across the sky.

It was the most beautiful sunset I could remember ever seeing.

And oddly enough, I could see the outline of the moon, too.

The sun and the moon all at once.

It was like the heavens aligned themselves just as nature splashed color across her canvas.

The waterfall was loud as the water splashed over the rocks.

I tilted my head up into the sunlight and closed my eyes.

I could feel just a touch of spray across my face as a gust of wind swept across the waterfall.

Feeling oddly enough at peace, I turned around, wanting to go up to the top of the waterfall before turning back.

I blinked rapidly. I'd been staring into the sun too hard.

A man stood a few yards away, holding the reins of a solid black horse with a white streak on his head.

It could not be. But it was.

It was Colton.

I was so overcome with joy that I couldn't move a single muscle, except I smiled.

And I could not stop smiling.

Even as he walked forward and took me in his arms, I couldn't stop smiling.

When he kissed me, I was still smiling.

"Hello Isabella," he said.

"Hi." I wrapped my arms around him and held on as he swung me off my feet to plant another, more serious kiss on my lips.

"How are you here?" he asked, letting me slide back onto my feet.

He entwined my fingers with his as we turned to walk back toward the house.

The sunset splayed out in front of us. The most beautiful sunset I had ever seen.

"How are you here?" I asked, not answering his question.

"I couldn't stay away," he said.

"Neither could I."

He kissed the backs of my fingers.

Something vibrated in his pocket.

"What's that?" I asked, startled by what sounded like a phone.

"It's your device," he said, pulling my phone out of his pocket.

"My what? My phone? I thought I had lost it."

"I kept it close to my heart," he said.

My hands trembled as he handed me the phone.

It wasn't supposed to work.

It was lit up, but it was locked on the camera.

I looked at Colton. "How long has it been doing this?"

"Just a few minutes. I looked at the sunset through it."

I played around with some buttons.

"Here," I said, holding the phone out in front of us for a selfie. I snapped a picture of the two of us with the sunset behind us.

Then I showed it to him and scrolled back to see the photo he had taken of the sunset.

That was it. None of the pictures I had taken before—in another time—were there.

Just the two pictures.

I did not know how long we would be able to look at the pictures… until the phone shut down again, but for as long as they lasted we had them.

"How does that work?" Colton asked.

"I don't know," I said. "It's not supposed to do this at all. It has no battery."

I tucked it back into his pocket. "I think you need to hold onto it," I said.

"Do you think it has some kind of magic?"

"I rather do now," I said as the path left the river.

Little blue daisies had sprouted up along the path and butterflies took full advantage of them.

It was starting to get dark though and we walked a little bit faster.

"I don't want to ever leave your side again," he said.

"I don't want you to." I was smiling again.

The house with its many chimneys, with wisps of smoke drifting out of each one, came into view.

"Whatever you do," he said. "Don't go down that road to Whiskey Springs again."

"You're just going to keep me prisoner here, then?" I asked. I had to ask, but I would honestly be content to stay here forever.

"Not so bad," he said. "Being a prisoner in a castle."

"Not so bad," I agreed. "I've had worse." I thought about my little apartment in Houston. My job.

That had been prison.

This was the opposite. This was freedom.

Wherever Colton was my heart would be free.

34

COLTON

"Let me see that again," Graham said, taking Isabella's cell phone again and turning it over in his hands.

Then he looked at Isabella. "This is not possible."

"I know," Isabella said. "But it is. How do you explain it?"

"I can't." Graham turned to his wife. "Do you know where my cell phone is?"

"Of course," Bailey said. "It's in your trunk. The one with the things you don't use."

He handed the phone back to Isabella.

"Zachary," he said. "Where is yours?"

"The same," Zachary said. "In a trunk."

"Come on," he said. "Let's get them. I have a theory."

The two men went upstairs to their respective rooms.

"What's he thinking?" Isabella asked me.

"I would not have a clue." I looked at my sister. "Bailey?"

"I don't have anything to do with any of this," she said, picking up Annabella by the fingers and swinging the baby from side to side.

"Dakota?"

Dakota lay on the sofa beneath a throw, her baby cuddled next to her.

It was her favorite position since she'd gotten pregnant.

She shook her head. "You'll figure it out. I'm sure."

I wasn't so sure we would. I maintained that it was indeed somehow magical.

According to Isabella, there was no possible way for her phone to work after being away from its charger for so long.

Yet it did. And it continued to work.

There were two photographs on it. Two of them that we could scroll through and look at.

She aimed the phone toward Bailey and Annabella.

Now there were three pictures.

The grandfather clock chimed the hour. It was late. Already eight o'clock, but no one seemed to notice.

A couple of minutes later, Graham and Zachary came back downstairs with their phones.

They both wore stunned expressions.

They held up their phones, both of them lit up.

It had been years since their phones had been charged, yet here they were. Lit up. Stuck on the photograph screen.

Graham took a picture of his wife and baby. Then what Isabella took what she called a selfie of the three of them.

Zachary did the same thing with Dakota and little Bradford, named after the Auclair siblings' father.

We laid the phones out side by side on the coffee table and studied them.

"Anybody have a clue?" Graham asked. "Isabella? You have the latest version. Is there anything new that would cause this?"

"Nothing I know of," Isabella said. "This should not be happening."

But it was. There was something magical about them.

We just didn't know what it was yet.

35

ISABELLA

The bright mid-day sun was hot on my head and was probably going to cause a sunburn, but I didn't care. I tipped my face up toward the sun and soaked in the rays.

It would be winter soon and cold. We'd miss the sunshine.

Bailey was in her studio painting while Graham read a book, never far from her side. Dakota sat in front of the fireplace doing her needlepoint. Zachary had an office in the house somewhere and he kept up with the accounts for everyone.

Colton and I sat side by side on the back lawn of the Daniel's House. We sat on a blanket, a picnic basket with lunch Benson had packed for when we got hungry behind us.

"Look through it, like this," Colton said, positioning the sextant in my hands.

I held the brass sextant in my hands and looked through it as he instructed.

"Okay," I said. "So now what?"

"Do you see the top of the mountain?"

"Yes." But with his hand on my shoulder, he was distracting me away from any coherent thoughts I might be having.

"So," he said, his voice soft in my ear. "Pull the lever like this until it lines up."

"And what is this going to tell us?" I asked.

"We can figure out the elevation of that tallest mountain across the valley."

"I think we can safely say that it's higher than we are."

"Don't you want to know how much higher?"

"Hmm." I handed the sextant back to him. "It's above tree line, so I'd say it's quite a bit."

"You're hopeless," he said, taking the sextant and looking through it himself.

I studied his strong jaw, covered with enough stubble to give him a sexy dangerous look.

Watching him, I leaned back on my elbows. I pointed toward Long's Peak.

"See that mountain over there with the beaver crawling up it?"

"What beaver?" He turned with his sextant.

"Not a real beaver, silly," I said, tapping the sextant for him to lower it.

"See, it just looks like a beaver."

"Huh. It kinda does. Long's Peak. You know somebody climbed it last year."

"Don't even think about it," I said, narrowing my eyes.

He turned and, smiling at me, leaned over and kissed me on the nose.

"Over fourteen thousand feet high. Thousands of people try to climb it every year. Less than half of them make it all the way. And almost a hundred people have died climbing it."

"It would be such an adventure to be that high," he said. "You could see the whole world."

I groaned. "It's like a siren calling out to people like you."

"People like me?" he asked, pulling me back to a sitting position and holding my hands. "You know what I think?"

"No. but I think you'll tell me."

"I think that if a man can marry a woman from the future, he can do just about anything he wants to."

"Who said anything about marriage?" I asked.

"You do want to get married, don't you?"

I looked blankly at him. "It seems like a man who has four sisters would know how to properly propose to a woman," I said.

I sat up on my knees and rummaged through the picnic basket. Men. Stubborn. And clueless.

I pulled the bottle of wine out of the basket and glanced over my shoulder. "How are we supposed to open—"

Colton was on one knee.

"You mean like this?" he asked.

I sat back and gaped at him.

It had been three weeks since Colton had come back to Graham and Bailey's house. There had been no talk of marriage. At least not where I could hear. Oddly enough, everyone acted as though we were married.

When he held out a hand, I put the bottle in it.

Smiling, he sat it aside and held out his hand again. I put my hand in his.

"Isabella Becquerel," he said, making my heart flutter. "I've known from the moment I first saw you that you were the one I wanted to spend the rest of my life with. And it should be noted that I was not looking for anyone to marry."

I smiled and blinked back tears of happiness.

"Isabella. Will you marry me? Will you do me the honor being my wife?"

"Yes," I said. "That's why I'm here."

"It's our fate to be together," he said. "I will always believe that."

"Me too." I nodded and wiped away the tears that spilled over my cheeks. Tears of happiness.

He pulled me into his arms. Kissed me on the lips.

"So," he said. "Let's plan a wedding."

A wedding.

I had gone all the way into the past to find the love of my life and it was real. No games.

36

COLTON

When I'd said we had to plan a wedding, I hadn't known exactly what I was getting into.

My sister, Bailey had grinned and gone straight away to her study. The next day Graham had gone into town to send what I learned shortly thereafter were invitations.

The following week, my sister, Andrea arrived with her husband and two children. Two days later, Elise and her husband arrived.

The huge house suddenly seemed not quite so very big.

I sat with Isabella on the back porch swing. The first moment we had had alone all day. The cool night air was alive with crickets and lightning bugs. And an owl hooted in a tree not so far away.

Isabella was nestled next to me, her feet up, arms wrapped around her knees.

"It doesn't seem fair to you," I said.

"What doesn't seem fair?" she asked, looking up at me.

"There are so many of us and only one of you."

She shrugged. "I had no family to come even if we were in the future."

"None?"

"None."

"Everyone has family."

"I don't," she said. "I'm the only child of two only children. My grandparents are gone and my parents live in France."

"France?"

"Yeah. I've never been there."

I nudged her forward so I could look into her eyes. "You do know that Vaughn was born in France, right?"

"I guess I did," she said. "But I hadn't given it much thought. What does it mean?"

"I don't know that it means anything. It's just… interesting."

But I was certain it meant something. Perhaps it spoke to Isabella being directly descended from Vaughn Becquerel.

"Do you miss them?" I asked.

"No more than any other child misses their parents."

"I miss mine," I said. "I wish they could have met you. They would have loved you."

"Yeah? I'm sure they would love your sisters' husbands too."

I swept the hair back off her cheek. "You especially," I said.

"Why is that?"

"Not because you're beautiful and charming," I mused.

She scowled at me.

"I mean, that helps," I said. "But because you're perfect for me."

"We're perfect for each other," she said.

Dakota came to the door. "Colton. Isabella. We need to show you something."

"What is it?" I asked, but she was already back inside. "I guess we're going inside now."

"The downside to living with family," she said.

I helped her stand. "Do you want us to get our own house?"

"Not unless you do. I love your sisters. I love living here with them."

"Good," I said. "I like it, too."

We walked inside, hand in hand, straight to the parlor.

All four of my sisters were sitting there with their husbands. And their children.

Five cell phones were lined up on the table.

"What's this?" Isabella asked.

"I don't know."

Leading her by the hand, we took a seat on the sofa.

Graham leaned forward and touched each phone, one by one and they all lit up.

Isabella squeezed my hand.

"They aren't supposed to light up like this.

"I have a couple of ideas," Zachary said. "I've been thinking about this."

We all looked at him.

"There's a thing called inductive energy… Never mind," he said when we all looked blankly at him.

"Maybe," he said, "the phones are working because they're all together. Or…"

"Or what?" I asked.

"Maybe it's because we're all together with our soulmates."

I grinned. Zachary might be from the future, but he was an alright kind of guy.

EPILOGUE

Isabella

November 1870
Three Months Later

It was the annual Daniels House Autumn masked ball.

Everyone in Whiskey Springs was invited.

Orchestra music filled the house as we all got ready to head downstairs in our ball gowns.

I wore a ballgown with a thousand yards of cascading velvet falling to the floor. The material was a lovely greyish mauve. In the future they would call it mountbatten pink. The material was even more than the blue gown they had given me before. The neckline dipped low, fashionably low, but it felt scandalous. Long white gloves covered my elbows in a demure contrast.

Anna, one of the ladies who had come to help us get dressed and do our hair had somehow entwined a matching pink ribbon in my hair I had chosen to tie together and pull around my left shoulder.

Walking toward the door of my bedroom, I passed a beautiful landscape painting Bailey had done just for me and Colton.

It was a painting of the sunset we had shared the evening Colton had come home. A wedding gift painted from the photograph he had taken with my cell phone.

The cell phones didn't work anymore. They had played their part, whatever it might be.

It didn't matter. Just being here was enough.

Colton and I had gone into Whiskey Springs by way of the river road. I had made it there and back without any hint of time travel.

So now we knew that we were not bound to stay here. We could go anywhere we wanted to go.

The thing was, there was nowhere else we wanted to go. Maybe later. It was definitely good to have options.

"You forgot your mask," Anna said, rushing forward to situate my greyish mauve mask over my eyes, letting the long ties hang down my back.

"You're going to make a beautiful bride," she said.

"Thank you."

It seemed like an odd thing to say, so I pondered her comment as I stepped out into the hallway and walked toward the stairs.

The music changed into a tune that teased the back of my mind.

Was I the last one to come downstairs?

The clock began to chime the hour. Six o'clock. I wasn't late and I wasn't early. I was incredibly punctual.

Nonetheless, it seemed I was the last one to come downstairs.

The moment I reached the top of the stairs, I saw Colton standing below, leaning against the banister.

He'd been waiting for me. We had been inseparable over the past few weeks.

When he smiled up at me, butterflies fluttered in my stomach.

I already knew he was the most handsome man here.

Tall, dark, and handsome came to mind.

And he was to be my husband.

I'd follow him to any time or place.

Keeping one hand on the banister and carefully maneuvering the skirts with the other, I reached the bottom where Colton was waiting for me.

"You looking stunningly beautiful," he said as I placed my hand in his.

"As do you."

The music changed again. I immediately recognized the wedding march, but…

I looked over at Colton. He just smiled.

Something wasn't like I expected.

Granted, this was my first masked ball, but everyone was looking at us.

Colton leaned close. "Just so you know, my sisters did this. And although I didn't actually come up with the idea, I had veto power. I think you'll be okay with everything."

"What…?"

"It's our wedding day," he said.

"What? I don't—"

Graham appeared at my side. "Can I have the honor of walking you down the aisle?" he asked.

Colton leaned close again. "I'll see you in a few minutes."

"Happy wedding day," Graham said, taking my arm. "Bailey and Dakota insisted on surprising you."

"It's definitely a surprise."

We took two steps.

He stopped. "Wait. I think this is where I'm supposed to unmask you."

"Already?" I asked as he untied the ribbon holding my mask and handing it to me. "You can use this later, I guess."

Dakota handed me a bouquet of roses.

"I'm a little overwhelmed," I said.

"Welcome to the family."

The walk down the aisle was not nearly as long as it seemed, but I was trembling the whole time.

When Graham handed me off to Colton, I settled.

This was right.

Everything was right.

The spell that had been spun so many hundreds of years ago, passed down from generation to generation, ran through my blood.

It had gotten me here to this very point.

Hundreds of years before I had been born, I had found my place.

And most of all, I had found my one true love.

My soulmate.

Keep Reading for a preview of
THE HEART OF CHRISTMAS...

Chapter 1
Jenna Garrison

Swiveling around in my ergonomically correct—and far too comfortable—office chair, I grabbed a book off the built-in bookcase behind me. A small paperback written by one of my favorite psychologists William Glasser.

I swiveled back around again and flipped through the highlighted and tattered pages of the thin book, looking for a quote about positive addiction.

I picked up my highlighter as a line of text caught my attention, snapped off the lid, and carefully highlighted the words in yellow.

It wasn't, however, what I was looking for, so I flipped forward a few more chapters.

I shivered. Maintenance must have already started turning the heat down in the buildings. It was cold outside, below freezing, and the window of my third-floor office was fogging over.

But the skies were clear and no snow in the forecast for the next week. Unfortunate for those celebrating Christmas in Pittsburgh.

My heavy dark gray wool coat, light gray cashmere gloves and matching scarf were great for here, but once I got to the mountains of Colorado, I would have to trade them in for one of the heavy down coats my grandmother kept on hand at her house.

I put the cap back on the highlighter and set it aside.

The elite, private university was quiet today—the Friday before Christmas break. The offices would be closing at noon today, nothing unusual for a Friday, but the buildings would be locking, too.

As a university professor, I could stay as long as I wanted to, of course, but by then it would be time for me to head to the airport. I was planning to leave my car parked here, on campus in the gated faculty parking area, and taking an Uber over to the airport. My car would be in a locked lot and it was so much easier than trying to find a parking spot at the crowded airport, especially this time of year.

My two fairly large hardback suitcases waited in the car. It was hard to pack light in the winter. I needed to allow for time to grab them before the Uber got here.

I checked the time again.

I wouldn't even be here today, except that my office was only a couple of miles from the airport. I glanced out the window as an outgoing jet passed, making its way into the sky. My stomach churned a little. I wasn't exactly a nervous flyer, but I wasn't exactly a giddy flyer either.

My flights consisted of once or at most twice a year to Denver and once to a national psychology conference wherever it happened to be. The last one was in San Francisco.

That had been a long flight. Literally across the country from Pittsburgh to San Francisco. I had actually slept some of that flight. My friend and colleague, Henry, had sat next to me on the flight, so that had made it tolerable.

Next summer's conference was going to be in New York. A short flight. And I was most definitely looking forward to seeing New York for the first time. Maybe as the Psychology

Club advisor, I could get a few students together to take with me. I could supervise them putting together a poster presentation.

The phone rang in the main office across the hall. It went to voicemail since the office assistant had taken the day off. Departmental policy.

Since I was working on my own research, I didn't count. Besides, we shared a floor with the biology department and they were all here. Having their Christmas party starting at noon.

They were different, the biology people. I guess since as the psychology department, we tended to think more about family and less about looking at bacteria through a microscope.

Already someone was fiddling with the music, landing on a popular festive tune. As I hummed along to myself, I realized I was actually looking forward to going to Whiskey Springs for Christmas. It almost always snowed in the mountains on Christmas.

Maybe I'd grab a sandwich on my way out. Maybe a cookie, too. It would be better than airport food.

Finding the quote I was looking for, I typed it into my document and hit save.

There. That was enough work until after the new year.

I had two weeks to spend with my grandparents and I would make the most of it. No work allowed. I wouldn't even take my computer. I would take my iPad, though, because I sometimes read fiction on it. I stashed it in my leather book bag along with the paperback romance novel I was halfway through.

My fingers brushed against an old greeting card that had gotten shoved into the bottom of my bag. I pulled it out and read the obligatory prose.

Thinking of you. Have a wonderful day.

Todd

I stared at it a moment. Tamped down the wave of feelings I had dealt with months ago.

Todd was no longer in my life. Not that we ever had more than a couple of dates anyway.

I had rather liked him. The part that stung more than anything else was that I had *told* people about him. I'd told my grandmother and a couple of my friends including Henry. I'd even mentioned him to my friend Simone in Colorado.

Taking a deep breath, I ripped the card in half. It felt good so I ripped it in half again. I kept ripping it up until I had a little heap of pieces on the desk in front of me.

There. That felt surprisingly good.

Cathartic.

I wasn't sure where that came from. I'd most definitely thought I was over Todd.

I was over him.

Definitely.

I saved my work, powered off my computer, and slipped the book back onto the bookcase.

It was time to go.

Time for Christmas in Whiskey Springs.

My favorite time of year.

Chapter 2
Daniel Fleming

Even for Houston, it was warm for late December. Hard to get in the Christmas spirit when it was seventy degrees outside.

Even with Post Oak lit up all the way down with synced Christmas lights. They almost—not quite, but almost—seemed out of place. I had a buddy whose wife dragged him to the Smoky Mountains every year for the holidays. Maybe they were on to something.

I sat in the cockpit of a little Cessna Skyhawk. A four-seat, single-engine airplane that belonged to my grandfather Noah Worthington.

This was, in fact, one of my grandfather's first personal airplanes. Not THE first. Grandma had insisted that he sell that one years ago. But definitely one of his oldest planes. He always winced when I called it vintage.

It was still a good-looking airplane. In fact, someone had just updated the Skye Travels logo splashed in red across the fuselage and sweeping up onto the tail.

Grandpa Noah had, in fact, just bought a new Phenom. I would love to get my hands on that one, but he either flew it himself or one of the more experienced pilots did. My uncles.

I flipped open my iPad, tapped my weather app, and checked the radar again.

I was a little compulsive about checking the radar, especially when I had a feeling the weather forecasters were missing something.

Most of us pilots were our own meteorologists. We had to be. Our lives depended on an accurate forecast of the weather. A pilot who relied completely on the weather forecasters ran the risk of not having a very long career. The saying went something like *there are old pilots there are bold pilots, but no old, bold pilots.*

But I was cleared by FSS all the way to Whiskey Springs. And my objective assessment had no argument.

I turned on the engine and watched the propeller start slow then vanish as it sped up.

Continued checking off the boxes on my pre-flight checklist.

Since I was traveling alone, I didn't have to be in any particular hurry. But being the Friday before Christmas—three days until Christmas in fact, the airport was bursting at the seams and I was already in the queue.

I put on my headset, blocking out some of the engine roar, and spoke to flight control.

Cleared to taxi to the runway.

I always got a little rush when it was nearing time to fly. No matter how many times I'd taken a plane up—nearly every day —in the last four and a half years, I still got that little thrill of adrenalin shooting through my veins every time.

Grandpa believed that was the sign of a true pilot. *Means it's in your blood.*

Grandpa definitely had flying in his blood, so he would know. He had started his own company, Skye Travels, years ago, before I had even been born. It had grown by leaps and bounds to the point where its reputation rivaled that of the major airlines.

As his grandson, I reaped the benefits of his success. I still had to do the work though. There were no shortcuts allowed. I'd proven my abilities in the cockpit, but I didn't have the experience yet to warrant taking the Phenom up.

One day. One day I would have the chance to fly the latest and greatest.

I went down the list, continuing to check gauges. Everything was in order.

My plan was to spend tonight and tomorrow night at the

Daniels House in Whiskey Springs. I would be home in time for Christmas.

To say that Christmas was a big deal in my family would be an understatement.

There were so many of us and we all gathered for Christmas Eve at Grandpa and Grandma's house. Grandpa Noah and Grandma Savannah had five children… six counting Noah's daughter by his first wife… and scores of grandchildren.

That left Christmas morning for families and Christmas day evenings for in-laws. It was a well-tolerated system.

Kinda left me in the wind on Christmas day, though, as a single man. I had yet to find the girl who would be my Christmas day family.

Mary Beth from junior high had been my last—only—great crush, but she had disappeared off the face of the earth after eighth grade.

No matter. I knew what to look for now. I would know when I felt that tug at the heart again.

I wasn't looking though. I didn't believe in all that swiping business.

I'd heard my Grandpa Noah and Grandma Savannah's story enough times that I knew how the heart worked. It happened when it happened.

But right now I was cleared for takeoff. It was time to fly.

Chapter 3

Jenna Garrison

DECEMBER *21*

. . .

WHISKEY SPRINGS and Christmas are synonymous, at least in my mind.

The streets glowed with a million strings of multi-colored Christmas lights, mostly blue, red, and green strung across the streets and down the poles. Mostly clear around the shop doors and windows.

Everything that didn't move got draped with a string of lights or garland or a wreath. Even some things that did move got caught in the festivity. Like the pickup truck that I parked next to on the side of the two-lane street. Someone had given the truck reindeer antlers.

I stepped out of my rented car and stretched. The drive from the Denver airport was long and was one of the primary reasons I only visited at Christmas.

I still had a thirty-minute drive left and it was getting dark.

Hence, the stop at the little designer coffee shop.

Christmas music echoed along main street, piped from speakers that covered the town from the savings and loan to the coffee shop to the antique store down the street.

There was a line and, it seemed, people taking more time to talk than to order. Definitely different from the city.

I used the time standing in line to text my grandmother.

ME: *In Whiskey Springs. Grabbing a coffee. Then will be on my way.*

GRANDMA: *Looks like roads might get icy. Be careful!*

"Next."

I gave the college student behind the counter my drink order and stepped aside to wait. Every year there was someone new behind the counter.

ME: *Don't worry. I'll be there before you know it.*

GRANDMA: *It's my job to worry.*

I sighed and didn't bother to tell her that worrying didn't help. I knew. I'd read the research.

"A large soy extra foam, three pumps of vanilla, peppermint mocha, extra hot cappuccino."

I slipped my cell phone into my handbag and grabbed my red to-go cup just as someone else wrapped his fingers around the cup, too. Our hands clasped together perfectly.

My fingers frozen on the cup, I looked up at the man, his hands clasped with mine, and immediately dubbed him Mr. Heart-throb.

My days were spent standing in front of a classroom of college students. And to be honest, between grading papers and preparing lectures, I didn't have much of a social life.

"I think this is my coffee," he said.

I smiled the smile that I used on students who thought they knew what they were talking about when they truly had no clue.

"I don't think so," I said. "I'm the only person who orders this."

He smiled back, looking at me with sparkling baby blue eyes. If he was going for that whole handsome business guy in a suit look, he had it nailed.

"A large soy extra foam, three pumps of vanilla, peppermint mocha, extra hot cappuccino." The barista set another cup on the counter and rolled her eyes.

"That's not possible," I said, mostly to myself.

Mr. Heart-throb and I looked at each other as he released my cup… and my fingers.

"Well," he said with a cocky grin. "You were here first."

After a quick roll of my eyes, I took my coffee and headed out the door to my car.

I had somewhere to be. I did not have time for thinking about the odds of ordering the exact same drink at the exact same place at the exact same time as another person, much less a guy who looked like him. And not just anywhere. The little town of Whiskey Springs.

Still stewing with the impossibilities of the situation, I got into my car and pulled out, only to have to stop at a traffic signal on the same block.

While I sat waiting for the light to turn green, I could not help looking in my rearview mirror. Mr. Heart-throb got into the pickup truck with the antlers.

I laughed out loud at the incongruence. Mr. Heart-throb business guy who ordered an ultra-designer coffee drove a pickup truck with antlers.

As I picked up my cup to drink, I saw the name scrawled on the side of the cup.

Daniel.

Well, Daniel. It appears that I'm the one who snagged *your* coffee.

My cell phone rang, coming through the car's speakers.

It was my best friend Henry.

"Someone sounds chipper," Henry said.

"I do not," I said.

But Henry just laughed. "It's about time. Maybe that clean mountain air will get your head out of those books and get your blood flowing again."

"My blood flows just fine," I said, trying not to sound testy, but he just laughed.

"I just wanted to make sure you made it okay."

"I'm in Whiskey Springs. Almost to the house. But I won't have phone service in a few minutes, so your timing was perfect."

"Well, text me when you get there," Henry said. "so I won't send out a search party."

"Will do," I said. "Give Bobby a hug for me."

"Consider it done."

Henry was my best friend who just so happened to have an office down the hall from mine. He honestly made office hours fun, so much so that we coordinated our schedules. A single parent since his wife passed two years ago, he had an adorable six-year-old boy.

We disconnected and I focused on the road. The drive from Whiskey Springs up the mountain to my grandparents' house was a steep, windy road that was could turn deadly with little to no warning.

Keep Reading THE HEART OF CHRISTMAS...